The Pleasures of Manhood

ILLINOIS SHORT FICTION

The Pleasures of Manhood

Stories by Robley Wilson, Jr.

UNIVERSITY OF ILLINOIS PRESS

Urbana   Chicago   London

"A Stay at the Ocean," *Carleton Miscellany*, Summer, 1969; reprinted in *EcoFiction*, ed. John Stadler (Washington Square, 1971).

"Saying Goodbye to the President," *Esquire*, February, 1974; reprinted in *SuperFiction, or the American Story Transformed*, ed. Joe David Bellamy (Vintage, 1975), and in *All Our Secrets Are the Same*, ed. Gordon Lish (Norton, 1976).

"Addison," *Antaeus* #24, Winter, 1976.

"The Apple," *Carleton Miscellany*, Winter, 1968; reprinted in *Three Stances of Modern Fiction: A Critical Anthology of the Short Story*, ed. Stephen Minot and Robley Wilson, Jr. (Winthrop, 1972).

"The *United States*," *Fiction International*, February, 1977.

"The Demonstration," *Carleton Miscellany*, Summer, 1970.

"On the Island," *Metamorphosis 1961*, April, 1961.

"Others," *Carleton Miscellany*, Fall, 1965.

"Visions," *Colorado State Review*, Spring, 1977.

"Happy Marriages Are All Alike," *Fiction International*, Fall, 1973.

Library of Congress Cataloging in Publication Data

Wilson, Robley.
 The pleasures of manhood.

 (Illinois short fiction series)
 CONTENTS: A stay at the ocean.—The pleasures of
manhood.—Saying goodbye to the President.—[etc.]
 I. Title.
PZ4.W7534Pl [PS3573.I4665] 813'.5'4 77-24216
ISBN 0-252-00665-8
ISBN 0-252-00670-4 pbk.

Contents

A Stay at the Ocean

On the sixth day of his vacation in the old house on Perkins Point, Stephen Bell woke, as usual, at five-thirty. The sun was on the wall opposite the small window of the bedroom, though the room was still chilly. Birds in the meadow behind the house made unintelligible conversation, and the remoteness of the ocean's noise suggested that the tide was out.

He got up and dressed. His wife, Clarice, was snoring becomingly in the big bed, and he paused on his way to the kitchen long enough to look into his daughter Linda's room and see her curly blonde hair nestled into the corner of one elbow. He felt a strong possessiveness toward both his women, and a kindness; he did not wake them.

In the kitchen he quietly poured himself a glass of orange juice, washed a vitamin pill down with it, then set out on his customary walk down to the sea.

The summer place, a modest white building the Bells had rented through an agent in Damariscotta, had been built in the 'Twenties nearly at the tip of the point. From its upper windows it provided a view of the Atlantic in three directions, and while the Point had very little sandy beach—only a strip of some hundred feet along the southwest edge—it had nearly three-quarters of a mile of shoreline along which Stephen could stroll in the early light. Rocks and split black ledges met the thrust of the sea with a kind of stubbornness, and brief reaches of lowland were strewn with coarse stones the ocean was rounding into its own toys. At the tip of the Point was something fairly worth calling a cliff; at high tide it dropped off five or six feet to the water; at low tide it became nearly impressive.

It was to the edge of this overhang that Stephen walked each day, to look at the sea and to assemble his private thoughts—this morning no different from any other. He noticed that the tide was remarkably low. Rocks he had never seen before had risen up off the end of the Point; his cliff plunged down not to green water, but to an unfamiliar shelf of darker stone which sloped gradually toward open sea. This morning the nearest tidal pool was so far away that it took all his strength to throw a stone hard enough to reach and ripple the smooth surface. Thrumcap Island, nearly a mile out, was an unaccustomed high shadow in the morning fog, and a few yards out from the tiny beach the blue rowboat which had come with the house sat aground on damp sand; the rope from its bow looked ridiculous, as if the boat were anchored somewhere under the earth.

"What's going on?" Stephen said, half to himself, but loud enough to startle a single gull overhead. The gull, which had appeared out of the fog, glided back into it. Stephen threw a last rock after it and returned to the house.

He found Clarice getting breakfast; Linda, in pajamas, had just poured a bowl of dry cereal and was now spilling a pitcher of milk over and around it.

"Did you get your pill?" Clarice asked.

"First thing." Stephen sat at the table across from his daughter. "You ought to see how low the tide is."

"The moon's full," his wife said. "It was low yesterday."

"I know, but this is *really* low. I've never seen anything like it."

Clarice set a plate of eggs before him. "Coffee's coming," she said. "Lin, please honey, eat over the bowl."

"You could walk halfway to Thrumcap," Stephen said.

Linda looked up from her cereal.

"No kidding, Lin. Halfway to Thrumcap."

"What do you suppose it is?" his wife said.

"Don't know," his mouth full. "What you said, I guess. The moon."

"Daddy, does the moon make tides?"

"So they say. Clarice? It's so low I can't throw a rock to the nearest water. And the boat's high and dry."

"How does the moon make tides?" Linda persisted.

"Gravity," Stephen said. He winked at his daughter. "But you know what I think? I think this tide is too low for the moon to take credit for. I think the ocean is just a gigantic swimming pool, and somebody's draining it."

"Mother, *is* the ocean a big pool?"

"I think your father's teasing you." Clarice poured two cups of coffee and brought them to the table.

"*You* swim in it, don't you?" Stephen said.

"Everybody does."

"There you are. It's a pool, and somebody's draining it, and now we can walk halfway to Thrumcap."

Clarice frowned at him. "Drink your coffee, and stop feeding misinformation to eight-year-olds," she said.

Stephen patted his mouth with a napkin and pushed his chair back. "You think I'm making it all up," he said. "You come on and I'll show you."

By the time Stephen had jogged down to the Point, the two women trailing after him, the fog had begun to burn away and Thrumcap Island stood monumentally ahead of them. The sea had receded still further; now over the mile between the Point and the island only a few round pools of water were left. All else was a waste of gray sand and flattened black weed. The island looked as if it had been lifted onto a plateau of sand, rimmed with twisted tree-roots.

Clarice stopped short. "Oh, Steve," she said. "Oh, Steve; my Lord."

"Is that something?" Stephen felt oddly as if he were taking credit for the phenomenon.

"Look at all the lobster traps!" Linda shouted.

Stephen looked. Where his daughter was pointing he saw a line of a dozen or so lobster pots mired in the channel about fifty yards out from the old shoreline. He started down the slope to the small beach.

"Let's have some lobsters," he called back.

"Steve, no. They belong to Paul Dunham."

He faced his wife. "But they'll just die, won't they? They won't be any good to anybody."

"Paul will get them."

"How? You can't run a boat through the sand."

"Then he'll walk. Stop showing your criminal side."

Stephen shrugged and came back.

"Aren't we going to have lobsters?" Linda said.

"We'll buy some, honey," Clarice told her. "Steve? Isn't this awfully strange?"

"I'll go along with that."

"I mean, this couldn't happen, could it? Are we just all having a dream?"

"You want me to pinch you?"

"Be serious, Steve." She sounded ready to cry.

He hugged her lightly. "I don't know, Clar. Yes, it's strange. It's impossible."

"Is it bad when the water goes so far away?" asked his daughter.

"No, Lin, it's just very funny. Very unusual and crazy." He looked at Clarice. "What do you want to do?"

"I don't know."

"Hey, I do. Let's all walk out to Thrumcap and explore. We've never done that before."

Linda danced. "Yes, let's."

"What if the tide comes back in?" Clarice said.

"Then we'll be marooned on the island and we'll hail a passing lobster boat."

"But if this is low tide—" Clarice hesitated. "What will high tide be like?"

"Slow. And we'll see it coming and run back to the house before it gets us." Stephen started down the beach. "Come on," he yelled, and his family followed after.

It was something like walking the edge of a usual beach, the sand packed hard, and the footprints of the three of them spreading into patterns of dryness as they walked. Except that there seemed no end to the beach. The sand was remarkably clean, Stephen noticed, with only random patches of seaweed beginning to dry in the sun, and here and there a mussel shell or a black crab half-buried. The sensation of actually walking to Thrumcap Island was eerie. He had never landed on Thrumcap—not even by boat. When they reached the island, he had to climb up to it, hand over hand, along and through the exposed roots of a tall pine, then reach down to pull Linda and Clarice ashore with him.

"It would be lovely to build a cottage out here, and just be isolated from everybody," Clarice said as they crossed the island.

"Would have been," Stephen agreed.

"Why say it that way?"

"I think the tide won't come back in. I think the ocean must be drying up, or changing its basin, or something."

"Are you serious?"

"I don't know. It doesn't make sense that this is just some fantastically low tide." They were standing now on the far side of the island, facing southeast. "Just look," he pointed out. "You can't even *see* the ocean."

He felt his wife's hand find his and squeeze hard. "I'm scared, Steve."

He put his other hand over hers. "Freak of nature," he said. "Let's walk back and see what's on the radio."

By the time they had started across to the Point, other figures were moving out from the old shore—men and women, and a few children; some of them were carrying picnic hampers. Dogs pranced around family groups or clawed and nosed at objects half-submerged in the sand. Not far from his own beach Stephen saw a lone man plodding toward a lobster trap, pulling a high-sided wooden child's wagon behind him.

"There's Paul," Clarice said. "Why don't you see what he knows about this? I'll take Lin up to the house and try to get some news."

They separated. Stephen caught up with the lobsterman. "Morning, Paul."

Dunham nodded to him. "Morning, Mr. Bell." He was a thin, fortyish man, needed a shave, had watery-gray eyes that looked out under a long-billed yachting cap. He had pulled on hip boots over his clothes; in the wagon Stephen could see a few lobsters moving sluggishly against each other.

"What's happening, Paul?"

"Can't say." He had come to the next of his string of traps, and had stooped to open it, drawing out a single lobster. He measured its carapace, then turned a perplexed look toward Stephen. "Don't know what to do with the damned thing," Dunham said. "Too small, but there's no place to throw the critter back to." He replaced the lobster in the trap and stood up.

"What's happened to the tide?" Stephen repeated.

Dunham gazed eastward. "Man up the coast told me it's gone out close to fifteen mile," he said. "Lives up on Pine Ledges. Owns a telescope."

"Will it come back in?"

Dunham picked up the handle of the wagon. "I got my waders on," he said.

Stephen made an awkward gesture of parting. "Happy fishing," he said, stupidly.

He met his women near the beached rowboat. "Anything?" he asked.

"There's nothing on the radio but bad music," Clarice told him. "We should have brought the little TV with us. What do you want to do?"

"Look what some people are doing, Daddy."

"Steve, they're driving cars out there," Clarice exclaimed.

It was true. Stephen could see a half-dozen automobiles moving out toward Thrumcap, and the Schumanns—whose cottage was a few hundred yards northeast of theirs—had actually piled into their truck-camper and had just now driven off the beach, threading between two grounded sailboats toward the east.

"Let's do that," Stephen said.

"Drive out *there?*"

"Why not? Obviously it can support the weight."

"It would be fun," Linda said.

"Of course it would. Let's pack a lunch and get into the car and go."

"But go where?" Clarice wanted to know.

"To the ocean," Linda said.

"Right. That's what this vacation is all about. We'll drive to the ocean."

Clarice finally agreed, and in an hour the Bell car, a white compact station wagon, was packed for the outing. Clarice had made sandwiches and filled a thermos with coffee. Stephen had put in a six-pack of beer, along with some hamburger and a carton of milk—all of it packed with ice in the metal chest. Linda had gathered together a careful selection of comic books and dolls. Almost as an afterthought, Stephen loaded the Coleman stove, and a five-gallon can of gasoline he had bought the day before for the outboard motor —explaining to his wife how unlikely it was that they would be able to find either firewood or a gas station on the ocean floor.

"All set?" They were in the car, Linda curled in the back on a thin plaid mattress.

"All set," the women chorused.

Stephen was pleased that everything was turning out so well—that what might in some families have become a fearful time, a kind of domestic disaster in the face of the unexpected, was now resolved into one more vacation side-trip. Even Clarice seemed relaxed, though commonplace misgivings still plagued her.

"Do we have enough gas in the tank?"

"I filled it yesterday," he reassured her. "Cruising range up to 500 miles."

"I hope nothing breaks down."

"Not a chance," Stephen said.

"Well," said his wife reluctantly, "just don't drive too fast."

It was easy to disobey her, Stephen discovered. The surface he drove on was unbelievably smooth, and though he once in a while was obliged to go around upjutting rocks or to avoid genuine islands that rose ahead of the car, the experience was very much like that of crossing a shopping-center parking lot—every destination reached by the straight-line distance, with no attention paid to lines painted by developers or highway commissioners. And the ride itself was luxurious; no bumps, no curves to speak of, the tires against the gray sand making a sound like skis on dry snow. The further he drove, the

fewer the obstacles became; even with the speedometer needle swaying between 70 and 75, Clarice made no protest.

Several cars passed him—none of them closer than ten yards—
and the occupants of each car waved joyously and called out to the
Bells.

"It's certainly a free-for-all," Clarice remarked.

"They're excited," Stephen said. "Nobody ever did *this* before."

"You couldn't even do this on television!" Linda shouted.

At the end of an hour-and-a-half of driving, Stephen was surprised to see a great number of cars—thirty or forty, he guessed—
lined up about a mile ahead. They were stopped; the people in them
had gotten out and were milling around.

"What's that all about?" Clarice asked.

"Maybe the road's washed out," Stephen suggested. He winked at
his wife.

"You're so damned funny," she said.

"I bet it's the ocean," Linda said.

"Hey, I'll bet you're right." He slowed down and eased the station
wagon to a stop between two of the parked cars. "Okay," he said,
"everybody out."

But it wasn't the ocean. Walking in front of the car, the three of
them found themselves at the edge of a steep bluff.

"Wow!" said Linda. "Look how far down it is."

It was more than 200 feet to the bottom of the bluff—not a per-
pendicular drop, but at a perilously steep angle from where they
stood down to what appeared to be a limitless dry plain. The cliff
consisted primarily of coarse rock, partly bare, partly encrusted with
green and white shell-things. Deep crevices between the outcroppings of stone were filled with sand. The plain below seemed entirely
of sand, and looked flat as a table top.

"We'll never get down there," Stephen said. He heard a touch of
awe in his own voice.

"Quite a sight, isn't it?"

The words startled him; he turned and found himself facing a
stranger—a middle-aged man with rusty hair and plump chins.

"Incredible," Stephen agreed.

"There's a couple of guys down the line say they're going to try and drive a Jeep down to the valley. I say they're batty."

Stephen nodded soberly. "I should think so."

"Me and the wife, we're going to head south from here."

"Why south?" Clarice was asking the question.

The stranger hesitated and put out his hand. "Excuse me, folks," he said. "The name's Allen. We're out here from Des Moines."

Introductions were exchanged. Mrs. Allen, a dowdy facsimile of her husband, joined them.

"We met this gentleman from New York," Allen told them, "says he used to study geology in college. He claims that if you drive a couple of hundred miles south—down near Cape Cod, he says—and then head straight east, you won't have to run up against this particular cliff. I don't know, but he claims he does."

"That's interesting," Clarice said.

"Says you can drive right out on this Continental Shelf he used to study about," Allen added.

Stephen looked at his wife. "Want to try it?"

"Are you and Mrs. Allen going to do that?" Clarice asked.

"Oh, yes; we surely are."

"What for?"

"Curiosity, mostly," Allen told her. He seemed reluctant to say more.

"And the treasure," Mrs. Allen put in.

"Treasure?" Linda was suddenly interested.

"Oh, well, yes, we sort of thought we'd look around for a little sunken treasure." Allen shuffled uneasily as he spoke. "You know, all those old ships that went down—oh, hundreds of years ago—and up to now nobody's been able to find 'em. We thought we'd keep an eye out. You saw that old hulk on the way here?"

"No, we didn't," Stephen said.

"Oh, we drove past it. Half-buried thing. No way to get inside it."

"But we've got shovels in the pickup," Mrs. Allen said.

Allen began drifting away with his wife. "We'd better get started," he told Stephen. "Have a safe trip."

"Steve? Does that make sense? Finding sunken treasure?"

He gave a small, noncommittal gesture with his arms. "At this point, I'll believe anything. How about eating? It's way past noon."

"But we haven't seen any old hulks," Clarice said.

"True, but it stands to reason there must *be* some. There ought to be a lot of Second World War shipping scattered around somewhere, too."

"We haven't seen anything, not even any dead fish, or those strange underwater plants you see pictures of. Why is that?"

He passed around sandwiches. "I suppose everything got buried under silt or swept out clean. This was some tide, you know."

They ate. Stephen sat on the fender of the car, the sandwich in one hand, a beer in the other. As he gazed out over the edge of the bluff he marveled at how far he could see, and how little was to be seen. The horizon—how far away? Twenty? Thirty miles?—was as unbroken as the rim of a plate. God knew where the ocean was, what it was doing, how long it would recede from them. He shook his head, as if to wake himself up. Off to his right, a young couple in white deck shoes was gingerly climbing over the edge of the cliff. He leaned forward to get a glimpse of the precipitous slope. The couple was picking black, withered plants out of a thin river of sand. They climbed back up, obviously delighted with what they had done. Off to his left, a small boy was sailing bottlecaps far out and down to the plain; the caps glided like odd birds. Where were the gulls and cormorants? he suddenly wondered. Following the elusive sea?

"Let's take that drive south," he said to his wife.

"Should we, Steve?"

"We won't get lost. I'll move in so we can see the shore on the way down."

"We ought to go back to the house first, don't you think? Maybe we should get the tent, and some more food."

"No," he said, "let's be really adventurous. There's food enough for breakfast, and we can sleep in the car if we have to."

It occurred to him as he backed the car around and set a course for the southwest that he had to go as far as he could—as if something in him insisted that he find the ocean. He rationalized the insistence in two ways: first, the ocean was what he had left Cleveland for, and he refused to be deprived of it after fifty weeks of slaving over his drafting board; second, he certainly wanted to be able to tell his friends, firsthand, what that Great Tide business had been all about. *I was there*, he could say. *I was part of it.*

"Now there's land in front of us," Clarice was saying.

He had been driving for two hours since lunch, making good time as before, except that there had been considerable cross-traffic to keep him alert—cars, campers, motorcycles, all moving madly east. He had kept the New England coast in sight most of the way—*the old coast.*

"Let's go ashore and see where we are," he said.

What he had in mind was to stretch his legs in some kind of normal place, to find restrooms and buy gas, to keep his ears open for any news sifted in from the larger world. The landfall turned out to be the Gloucester peninsula, and Stephen was able to drive up out of the ocean bottom across a pebbled beach not far from a paved highway. In the nearest town he pulled into a gas station. Reading a road map while a sullen young man filled his tank, Stephen concluded that the town was Rockport, and he tried to estimate—referring to a sun that was by now halfway down the sky—which direction to set out in to avoid driving into Cape Cod Bay.

In twenty minutes they were on their way southeast; the attendant had refused to honor his credit card—another driver at the station had complained loudly—and Stephen had paid what seemed an unusually high price for the gas. *Frightened*, Stephen decided; *taking the cash while he can.*

He drove casually and fast; he was getting used to this sort of travel, to the experience of other cars strewn as far as the eye could see in every direction.

"It's something like an old-fashioned land rush," he said to Clarice.

"I suppose," she said. "Did you hear any news at the gas station?"

"Rumors, is all."

"Well, like what?"

He pursed his lips. "Silly things. Some guy told me he'd heard most of Europe was under water."

"My God, Steve."

"Oh, come on, Clar. That's hardly likely, you know."

"I *don't* know." She slouched into the corner by the door. "The water must have gone somewhere."

"Believe anything you want. Maybe it's Judgment Day."

His wife kept quiet.

Of course it was possible—that wild story about Europe. It was strangely logical, Stephen admitted. Still, fantastic. How could you explain it? A shift in the magnetic poles, maybe. Or a meteor—something huge—hitting the earth with incredible force. But wouldn't there have been earthquakes? He mused, scarcely thinking about his driving—not needing to. There were no obstructions, nothing to slow down for.

"I can't say much for the scenery," he said.

"Daddy, my stomach hurts," Linda complained.

He glanced at his watch. It was after six o'clock, he was amazed to notice; he had lost track of time since leaving Rockport, and surely his daughter had a right to be hungry.

"Be patient, honey," Clarice said in a tone part soothing, part mocking. "Daddy will stop as soon as he finds a nice shady spot."

He smirked. "Now *that's* funny," he said, yet almost at once he was startled to see something black on the horizon. He pointed. "What do you suppose that is?"

"I don't know," Clarice said, "but let's stop there."

Closer, he identified the object.

"There's our first shipwreck," he said. It looked, as he drew toward it, to be a modern ship—metal hulled, at any rate—stern up as if it had dived sharply to the bottom. Second World War? Victim of a submarine? Its enormous square plates were deep red with rust, and its unexpected presence made the miles of sand around it all the more desolate. Circling to the ship's shady side, he saw that two other cars were already parked alongside it.

"Company," he said.

"That's good," Clarice decided. "You'll have somebody to talk to while I get supper."

Stephen parked and got out. People from one of the cars had spread a cloth under the lengthening shadow of the hulk. A man appeared on top of the wreck and peered down over the crusted railing, hanging on to keep his balance against the rake of the deck.

"Looking for the ocean?" he called down to Stephen. "It's all in here." He pointed toward the submerged bow. Leaving the women to fix the hamburgers, Stephen walked around the ship and made his way precariously up the steep deck. "I think it must have been a tanker," the man above him said.

"Torpedoed?"

"I expect so." The man wore Bermudas and a Hawaiian shirt; he grinned at Stephen. "Makes you feel like Davy Jones, doesn't it? I looked into that hatch down there. Couldn't see anything, but I could hear water sloshing. Bet there's a lot of bones rolling around in there; poor bastards."

Stephen nodded. He didn't feel like talking, but stayed on the ship, bracing himself against a ventilator. To be above the ocean's floor was pleasant; the air was warm and windless; he even enjoyed the difficulty of keeping his balance, after hours of cramped driving.

Certainly this had been the most remarkable day of his life—of all their lives—and filled with small wonders. The lobsterman pulling his coaster wagon. The foolish couple from Iowa with their shovels and dreams of treasure. The boy and girl at the cliff, acting like honeymooners picking edelweiss in the Alps. And the ocean. The ocean he had grown used to in summer after summer of holidays in Maine—suddenly turned into a desert. Still— He felt a faint shiver of apprehension. If there was water in the hold of this broken tanker—

He edged his way to the open hatch, a gaping black hole in the rust and scale of the deck-plates, and tried to see inside. It smelled like ocean, he thought. He listened, and could hear the water. *Why should it be moving?* Stephen stepped off the hulk and looked around. Nothing—but was that fog, far off to the east?

Stephen called up to the man in Bermudas. "Do you hear anything?"

"No," the man said. Stephen noticed a car, about a mile away, headed west. "Wait a minute," the man said. "I do hear something."

It was the sound he had awakened to that morning—of the tide, far, far out.

"By George," the man said, "I think we've found her at last." He stumbled down from the deck. "We've caught up with her," he said, and went to tell his family.

Stephen walked back to the women.

"Not ready yet," Clarice said. "Why don't you open a can of beer?"

He took a deep breath. "Listen, I think we'd better start back. It's about a hundred-and-fifty miles to the Cape, but we ought to be able to get there just after dark."

Clarice tensed. "What is it?" she said.

"I just think we'd better go. It's been a long day."

His wife turned off the stove and dumped the meat onto the sand. "Linda, get in the car."

"Don't we get to eat anything?"

"Linda, honey, don't quibble with me." She glanced around. The two neighboring cars were gone. Other cars appeared from the east and sped past.

"I'm going to put that spare gasoline in the tank," Stephen said, "just so we won't have to stop."

As he worked, he could hear the soft, incessant whisper of waves at his back. He made a botch of pouring the gas. *Steady*, he told himself. *It's your own damned fault.*

When he finished, the women were inside, waiting. He tossed the gasoline can away in a high, tumbling arc, and hurried to get into the car. The sea noise behind them was by now so loud that he could hear it even above the engine as it burst into life. He shifted into first gear and skidded forward.

"Tides come in gradually, don't they?" Clarice said in a tight voice.

"Usually," Stephen said. He threw the shift lever into second; again the rear wheels of the station wagon spun, as if the sand under them were getting wetter.

"I just can't believe any of this," his wife said. She leaned her head against the back of the seat and closed her eyes.

Now he was in high gear. The engine was turning over smoothly and the speedometer needle stood unwaveringly at seventy miles an hour. Ahead of him the evening sun was sliding down to the horizon; he kept the car headed toward it, squinting across the enormous reach of gray sand. *What a queer thing*, he thought. *What a devil of a way to finish a vacation.* He was aware all around him of other cars, other drivers, all racing west on this incredible aimless track. One car passed him, then another, and he pushed the accelerator down. He overtook a white camper and swerved around it; the station wagon fishtailed slightly.

"What's the matter?" His wife opened her eyes.

"Nothing's the matter."

"We won't run out of gas now, will we?"

"Not a chance." He watched the needle slide past eighty. The sand was glistening ahead of him, water seeping to the surface. The tide must be racing in behind them. Could they swim free? Where would they swim to?

"Daddy!" The scream startled him. "Daddy, I can see it! I can see it coming after us!" Linda wasn't crying. In the rearview mirror he could see her face, half-turned in his direction, her eyes vivid, her mouth working desperately to make more words. Out the back window he could make out a low gray wall that seemed to be gaining on him. Under his wheels he could hear water splashing, see spray flying. He switched on the wipers.

He reached over and squeezed his wife's hand. *At least we're all together*, he thought. Off to the right he saw an overturned car, two men and a woman out trying to turn it upright. The sun was almost at the horizon and its light cast back a hundred rainbows through the wakes of a hundred cars. A pale, pebbly mist began forming on surfaces inside the car. The roar of the impossible tide was deafening; it seemed now to be all around him, and the deepening water drummed like hammers against the metal under the car. He was thinking irrelevantly of how quickly the salt sea would rust out the fenders and rocker panels when he heard Clarice for the last time, shrieking:

"Drive, Steve, drive. For pity's sake, drive, drive, *drive!*"

The Pleasures of Manhood

Warren March is standing in front of the bathroom mirror, shaving with his new electric razor. The sensation pleases him—the thrum of the shaver motor against the bone of his jaw, the vibration in his hand as if he has captured a giant bee. When he is finished, and switches off the razor, the stillness lets him down; distantly, he hears the television set blaring in the living room, knows that the noise is broadcasting out the opened windows of the apartment, carrying color cartoons of domestic life from Morningside across to the rain-gray tenements of Harlem.

He bows into the medicine-chest mirror. When he rubs his hand against the grain, the secret of his beard reveals itself to his palm. Still, the eye is deceived. He takes the small, stiff brush from the razor case and pokes it into the heads of the machine; powdery minor explosions result. He packs his instruments away, slaps on lotion, leaves the bathroom. In the hall, on the way to the bedroom, he pauses to survey his wife as she lounges on the couch before the television set.

"Why don't we take Alec out to dinner?" he says to her.

Carla March pushes her hand up under the back of her hair and lets a fall of black hang over her wrist. Without looking around, she says:

"Why bother? Why not just sit around and watch a show or something?"

"No, come on," Warren insists. "We can watch television any time."

Carla shrugs. "He's *your* best friend." She crosses her legs and dangles one shoe from the toes of her furthest foot.

"What's the matter with you?" Warren says.

"I'm thirty-one."

"That's a stupid answer."

"Look at the question."

"Every time Alec comes here, you start playing the old witch with me." Warren wants to say: *What am I going to do with you?*

Carla kicks off the shoe. "Why don't we have a go at charades, instead of eating out? I'll do Hansel and Gretel for you."

"You can't be two people at once."

"Tell that to my psychiatrist."

"You don't have a psychiatrist."

"I made him up." She twists herself to look at Warren, her chin resting on the back of the couch. "You aren't very handy at games anymore," she says.

Warren goes on to the bedroom, where he puts on a white shirt and selects a plain brown tie. He would prefer to go out to a restaurant for Saturday dinner, but it is true—what he has suggested in the living room—that Carla turns remote and unpredictable during the two or three times a year when Alec visits them. After eight years of being married, Warren will no longer believe in the persistence of old rivalries; what Carla does is rooted in something he can't explain. He ties his tie twice before he gets length to the proper end.

Finished dressing, and with his raincoat over one arm, he stops again in the living room doorway.

"I'm off to meet him," he tells his wife.

Carla rolls over on her stomach and closes her eyes.

"Keep in touch," she says.

Warren hurries out of the apartment, but on his way downtown he determines to return home slowly, to allow Carla time to put on a brighter mood. In Grand Central, he stands back from the gate where the Boston train is to arrive, idling time. He pushes his hands deep into the pockets of his raincoat; he whistles and shifts his weight from one foot to the other.

Doors begin to open and close. Alec appears, as tall and thin as ever, his coat draped over one arm and a scratched briefcase in his left hand. He greets Warren with a gesture of the coat.

"How's the professional student?" Warren says. He puts his arm around Alec's shoulders and walks him away from the gates. "How's the Ph.D. business?"

"Dull, to both questions," Alec answers. "How's Carla? How's the city?"

"Same answer," says Warren. He steers Alec out of the station. "I left Carla watching television."

As they walk, Warren thinks how they must look truly like old comrades. They sit in the front car of the Shuttle, facing the aisle. Warren becomes absorbed in a placard offering up for adoption a sad-eyed Asian child.

"Let's stop for a couple of drinks," he says.

They get off the train and climb up into the drizzle of Times Square, Alec pulling on his coat while Warren carries the briefcase for him. In a small, narrow bar the two of them order bourbon and water.

"Got a job yet?" Warren asks. Other questions have occurred to him—*Do you ever miss your wife? What's the matter with Carla?*—but he avoids them.

"Not yet. I've got an interview coming up."

Warren smiles over his glass. "You should be out in the world."

"I don't know if I could stand it," Alec says. "It would be like growing up."

"Teaching full-time has its rewards."

"Real wages."

Warren shakes his head. "No, I mean more than that. My students bought me an electric razor for my birthday."

"So you can think of them in the bathroom? Touching." Alec finishes his drink and waves off the bartender.

"Well, let's go," says Warren.

They take the train to 116th Street and walk to the apartment in the rain. By the time they arrive, Carla has changed her clothes. She has put off the gray slacks and the old black sweater in favor of the deep blue dress with the belt—a gift from her mother last spring—

and Warren notices she is wearing the silver brooch Alec once sent her from Copenhagen. The pin has never made him feel any husbandly jealousy. He has only just opened the door and motioned for Alec to enter when he senses the dryness in the apartment—the thinness of atmosphere—which always surrounds the three of them. The television is blank; the room seems neater than when he left it. Carla is waiting at the door.

"Alec," she says; pleasure is in her voice. She steps forward to take Alec's two hands in hers. Warren picks up the briefcase and nestles it on the floor against the back of the couch.

"We stopped for a drink on the way home," Warren says. He hears Carla saying:

"A new face is nice. You're a fresh pair of eyes to watch television with."

"She's on one of her sarcastic streaks," Warren explains.

"How's my favorite past?" Alec says to Carla.

Warren feels momentarily uncomfortable for them all. He takes off his raincoat, accepts Alec's. While he is hanging up both coats he listens to the talk behind him.

"How was the train ride?" Carla asks.

"The trip gets longer and longer. Can you put up with me overnight?"

"Can't you stay until Monday?"

"No, I have to meet an early class Monday morning."

Warren goes back to the living room. "How about a beer?" Without waiting for an answer he gets three cans from the refrigerator. He sets them, clattering, on the coffee table.

"I'd like an opener," Carla says.

"You don't need an opener for these."

"I'm a delicate hostess," she says. "I don't care to bloody my fingers on those damned salt spouts."

Warren finds an opener. The three of them sit around and sip the beer. Warren has taken a place on the floor, facing the other two, who have chosen opposite ends of the couch; he feels chill trickles of sweat down his sides. He can think of nothing to say.

"I made up a pretty good supper," Carla offers. "There's cold roast beef, and a little wine left over from last night."

"It'll be the best meal I've had in five months," Alec tells her.

Carla begins snapping a fingernail against the side of her beer can. Warren tunes himself to listen for the lowering pitch as she drinks.

"I ought to shave," Alec says.

"Why?" Carla wants to know.

"I feel grubby. Don't I look grubby?"

"Why not sit at table all unkempt and scholarly?"

Alec shrugs. "All right."

Carla's nail strikes deeper notes.

"Do you see much of Marian?" Warren asks Alec. It is a conscious unkindness.

"No, not since last April. She sent the boys up to spend the last two weeks in July with me at the Cape."

"How are they?" Carla asks.

Alec looks amused. "Grown-up and scary."

"Think you'll ever get married again?" says Warren.

"Who knows?"

Carla glares at Warren; he looks down to his beer, then up at the windows. The day is beyond dusk, and rain is glistening down both faces of the window that is still swung open.

"Why don't we eat?" Carla wonders.

Supper is quiet. Warren thinks he is beginning to feel relaxed. As the three of them finish the wine, Alec says to Carla:

"Do you remember that time Warren and I visited you in Norwalk?"

"When was that?" Warren asks.

"You know; years ago."

Carla giggles. "I was still at Conn, and you two were down from Bowdoin on your way to New York. Remember, Warren?"

"I guess so." He does.

"It was a Sunday afternoon," Alec says.

"And I offered you something to drink." Carla lifts her wine glass and almost chokes into it. "I offered Alec scotch or bourbon."

"And all you offered Warren was a glass of ginger ale."

They laugh; Warren scowls. He sees a stunning image of the sun-porch of Carla's home, of wicker furniture, of Carla pointedly atten-tive to Alec. Of Alec already preparing to use the afternoon for this revenge against Warren's reminder of his divorce.

"What's for dessert here?" he says grimly.

Afterward, Carla is the first to leave the table.

"Well, let's see what's on," she says.

The three of them watch a late movie and talk idly over the com-mercials. Before the movie has ended, Alec falls asleep on the couch. Shushing Warren, Carla unlaces Alec's shoes and finds an old blue blanket to put over him.

Warren watches her from the hall. "Tender, aren't you?" he re-marks.

"Shut the hell up," she answers.

Quite early Sunday morning Warren comes into the kitchen and pours himself a glass of orange juice. As he drains the tumbler he hears voices and goes back to the hallway. At the end of the hall he sees Carla, wearing her orchid-colored peignoir and leaning in at the opened bathroom door. Beyond her, Warren sees that Alec is pre-paring to shave, muddling the soap in his shaving mug with a wet brush.

He hears Carla ask: "What's that stuff?"

"Lather," Alec says. "This is shaving soap."

"I haven't seen anybody use that in years," she says. "My father used it when I was a little girl. He used to poke suds on the end of my nose when he got tired of me watching."

"Better stand back." Alec begins lathering his face.

"I like it." She watches him quietly for a moment. "What does it feel like on your face?"

"Hot and comfortable. It's very delicate and very nice, and some-times I wish I could leave it on."

"Warren uses an electric razor; some of his students gave it to him."

"So he said."

She watches him spreading the lather. "You've got it on your ear lobes," she giggles.

"It's the Van Gogh in me."

"How do you keep from getting it in your mouth?"

"Like this." He faces her, with his lips turned under against his teeth.

"It's like putting on lipstick," she says.

Alec sets the shaving soap aside; he rinses the brush and places it upright on the glass shelf over the sink.

"Why is it," Carla asks suddenly, "that it's so much fun to be a student, and so damned boring to be a teacher?"

"You're asking the wrong student."

"You know what I mean."

"No," Alec says flatly. "Why keep talking about it?"

At the other end of the hall, Warren coughs. "'Morning," he says.

"Hi, Warren," Alec says.

Carla half turns to him. "I'll start breakfast in a couple of minutes."

"No hurry," Warren says. He walks closer to the bathroom, still carrying the empty juice glass, seeing what Carla in the thin clothing looks like between him and the light.

"What's that?" Carla asks Alec.

"This is the razor," Alec says. He opens it and tips his head, setting himself to shave.

"It's not a safety razor, is it?"

"It's a straight razor."

"I thought it was different," she says. "I use a safety razor for my legs, and yours is different."

"Warren used to have one of these," Alec tells her.

"Did you, Warren?" She looks at him, seeming interested.

Warren frowns, thinking what he ought to answer.

"You bought a Rolls when we were in Europe, didn't you?" Alec says, absorbed in his shaving.

"I guess I did, but I never used it."

"I thought a Rolls was a car," Carla says.

"It's a razor, too," Alec says, "and a very good one."

"Don't you have it any more, Warren?"

"It's in the bottom drawer of the dresser," Warren admits. "I never used it. I was going to give it away, but I never got around to it."

Carla looks quizzically at her husband. "Aren't you queer," she says, and then turns back to watch Alec.

"Electricity is faster," Warren says, not directing the remark at either of them.

"It must be nice to be a man," Carla says, watching Alec put the finishing touches to his chin. "It must be nice to have something so pleasant to do to your face."

Alec laughs and winks over Carla's head at Warren. Warren feels himself return a foolish—ignorant—grin.

"What about it, Warren?" Alec rinses the razor and lays it, open, on the shelf. "Let's show her."

"Show me what?" Carla says.

"What?" echoes Warren.

"What it's like to shave. We'll give her the works; hot towel, after-shave lotion, the works."

"I don't know," Warren says. He wonders if Alec is serious.

"We'll just pretend we're barbers, and set up shop in the kitchen. She can be our first customer."

Warren hesitates. "Carla's not much on make-believe," he lies.

"Oh, come on," she says. "After eight years?"

Alec gathers up his shaving things. "Hippety-hop," he commands.

The three of them troop into the kitchen. Alec pulls one of the chairs out to the center of the floor and Carla sits in it looking flushed and nervous, pushing stray threads of hair back from her forehead. On Alec's instruction, Warren brings a yellow bath towel from the linen closet and drapes it under her chin. She surveys herself ruefully.

"Orchid and yellow," she says. "I look like a bed of irises."

Alec turns to Warren. "Can you find us some towels that aren't fluffy?"

"Dish towels. Sure," Warren says. He digs some out of a lower drawer beside the sink and straightens up. "What now?" he asks Alec. The bending and coming upright have made him slightly dizzy.

"Hot water. As hot as you can get it." Alec begins sharpening the razor.

Hearing the slock-slock-slock of the razor, Carla tries to see what is happening. "What's that noise?"

"Just honing the blade."

"You'll cut me."

"I'd cut you if it was dull," Alec says.

Warren wrings the towels under the hot water steaming from the tap. He gives them to Alec and Alec takes them to the chair.

"What are you going to do?" Carla wants to know.

"These go on your face. They condition the skin."

"They won't wreck my complexion or anything?"

"Of course not." He looks at Warren. "Will they?"

"Don't ask me," Warren says. He feels giddy.

"I'll leave a place for her nose to stick out, so she won't smother."

"I'd better *not* smother," warns Carla's muffled voice.

At the kitchen sink, Warren confers with Alec in a low voice.

"What are you going to do, exactly?"

"Don't worry," Alec says. "I'll use the back of the razor. I won't cut her."

"No, listen," Warren whispers, "she'll know if you do that. Really do it."

Alec hesitates, the tap water dribbling into the shaving mug in his hand. "What?"

"Really," Warren whispers. He realizes he is gripping Alec's arm. "With the sharp edge. Really do it."

Alec makes suds in the white mug. "Okay," he tells Warren. "Okay, you can take the towels off."

With the brush poised in his hand he confronts Carla, whose face glows pink and whose eyes are wide.

"Ready?"

"It won't hurt?" she says.

"It won't." He lays the lather on in soft, slow strokes. "Put on lipstick," he says, and puts the soap around her mouth when she obeys. "There. I got a little in your hair, but it's only soap and it'll wipe away."

Carla sighs. "Oh, it's beautiful. It feels like soft hands all over my face."

"Razor," Alec commands, and Warren places it in his outstretched hand. "Let me have one of those towels, too."

"Don't you cut me," Carla warns. Warren sees that, like him, she is trembling, but her eyes are uncommonly bright.

"Wouldn't dream of it," Alec says. He makes an elaborate show of testing the keen edge of the blade against his thumb, then glances oddly at Warren and goes to work. Warren catches his breath. The blade sends a sliver of light dancing across the walls and ceiling.

"What a curious sound it makes," Carla says weakly.

"Don't move. You'll make me slice you," Alec threatens.

She is dutifully quiet until he finishes and wipes the shreds of soap from her face and throat. Then she springs out of the chair and skips into the hall.

"I have to find a mirror," she calls back. In a moment she returns. "And I don't even look any different," she says.

"I hope not," Warren says, but he thinks she does.

"I feel marvelous. I feel all bright and new." She puts her fingers to her cheeks and looks from Warren to Alec. "How lucky to be a man and do this every day."

Warren laughs nervously.

Carla purses her lips and kisses Alec beside the mouth. "I'll get busy with breakfast," she says. Warren realizes she is still excited by the game.

After breakfast, as soon as Alec has left to catch his train, Warren goes to the bedroom. From the bottom drawer of his dresser he takes a small cardboard box. Opening it, he lifts out the Rolls razor he has bought nine years earlier at an army post exchange in England. Its case still glistens in his hand, but when he swings out the blade of the razor he finds faint prints of rust have appeared near the hinge. He carries it to the living room. The television is on; Carla is standing at the window, looking out. She scarcely turns her head.

"What's that?" she asks.

"The razor. I wondered what sort of shape it was in."

He goes to the kitchen and comes back with a rag and a can of sewing machine oil. Then he sits cross-legged on the carpet with the razor in front of him. He hears Carla's peignoir rustling behind him.

"It was the nicest visit we've ever had with Alec, wasn't it?" she says.

"I think it was," he agrees.

"I'm still tingling," she says.

She kneels beside him; he notices the lingering masculine odor of Alec's shaving lotion, how it is an aura which envelops her. As he begins working patiently at the disuse on the bright mirror of the razor he catches in her eyes a languid, unsettling interest.

Saying Goodbye to the President

We are strolling in the Rose Garden at dusk. The sky is clouded, taking on the first glow of lights from the Washington night, the traffic sounds muted by the rustling of a warm wind in the White House trees. The President walks with his hands clasped behind his back, his head bent slightly, scuffing at bits of gravel with the toes of his shoes. Behind us, at a little distance, two Secret Service men follow, talking discreetly, keeping their eyes on us.

I am the one who finally speaks, breaking a silence that has surrounded us like a smoke since dinner.

"I never thought it would end this way," I say.

"No," he says. "Neither did I."

"I'll miss you."

He grins—a flicker of his mouth so slight as to be almost an inward grin. "We had good times," he says.

We turn off the path and move across a damp lawn. The agents trail us at their interval, seeming careful not to step where we have stepped, avoiding the dark places in the grass that mark where we have pressed the dew against the earth.

"I suppose you're all packed," I say.

"Almost," he says. "A few pictures . . ." His voice falls; he finishes the sentence with a movement of his shoulders.

"I guess we'll both get over it."

"Things have a way of settling themselves."

"Will you think of me?"

"Can you imagine me forgetting?"

"Then I can live with this," I tell him.

He puts his right hand on my shoulder. "Try not to dwell on it," he says.

"All right," I tell him.

He signals to the agents. I turn away and begin walking rapidly in the direction of the traffic noise. I have given my oath I will not show tears.

We are at Key Biscayne, in a room whose two windows look across a deserted beach to the ocean. The President is standing, shoeless and shirtless, at one of the windows. It is daybreak; the sun streams around him and turns the room gold. He waves absently to a Secret Service man seated at the base of a palm tree, and with his other hand rubs at the gray hairs on his chest.

"They'll miss you," I say to him.

He sighs. "I suppose they will."

"They loved you the way a family would."

"They did—for a while, at least. I'll always have that."

"You've settled everything?"

"Oh, yes," he says. "All packed, ready to go."

He moves from the window and picks up a white shirt from the chair beside the bed. He draws it on carefully, the motions of his dressing like those of an old man.

"Can I help with the cufflinks?" I ask him.

"No, no," he says. "I can manage."

I stub out my cigarette in the glass ashtray. "Then I think we'd better get on with it." I stand up.

"Just let me put on my shoes," he says.

While he sits on the edge of the bed, slipping on the shoes, I button and adjust my jacket. I say: "It's going to be a scorcher"—not because I care, but because I am embarrassed and wish to say something.

The President nods, stands, scoops up his coat. At the door of the room I put my hand out to him. His mouth hardens.

"I think we can do without those, can't we?" he says.

"Yes, sir," I say, and follow him out through the bedlam of photographers to the waiting van.

We are aboard the *Sequoia*. It is a starless night; a light breeze is blowing over the mouth of the Potomac and there is no sound save the low murmur of a foghorn. The President is kneeling at the rail of the yacht. He wears a wetsuit, goggles pushed up from his brow. He is checking the pressure of his air tanks. When he talks, it is in a voice scarcely louder than a whisper, and the words come fast upon one another. The *Sequoia* rocks gently in the rising tide.

"You've got it all straight?" the President says.

"Yes, sir. Trust me, sir."

"All right." He hoists the tanks onto his back. I help him adjust the fastenings. He takes the airpiece into his mouth, checks the tanks one last time.

"Good luck," I tell him.

"Thanks. Remember—not a word to anyone."

"Right."

"You won't hear from me for two weeks, but don't worry. Everything's arranged. In thirteen days, mail the package to Cuernavaca; in twenty-seven days, mail the large envelope to Caracas." He pulls down the goggles. "After that, you'll get instructions every two weeks."

"Yes, sir."

He shakes my hand. "I'm counting on you," he says. The next moment he has slipped over the side of the yacht—a dim wake phosphorescent from the ship's lights. Then a crewman appears at the rail beside me.

"What's up?" says the crewman. "I thought I heard a splash."

"You did," I tell him. "The President just fell overboard."

The crewman lights a cigarette. "No kidding?" he says. He offers me a Kool from his pack. We smoke in silence.

We are at Camp David, in a large clearing not far from the main compound. The balloon is not yet inflated; it is laid flat on the grass, nearly a hundred feet long, striped blue and white. The staff is milling about. The President is in earnest conversation with the Secretary of State. Two men in overalls are fussing with the burners, while a third man is loading the gondola.

I am standing just close enough to overhear the President.

"You've booked passage?" the President is saying.

"I have," the Secretary answers.

"Capital," says the President. "Now you'll probably lose sight of me somewhere along the north shore. You know what to do."

The Secretary nods.

I drift to the edge of the field. The balloon is being filled, the great bag beginning to tug at its shrouds, men arranged in an oval seeing to it that the balloon expands evenly. In another twenty minutes the balloon is full, bulging in the afternoon sunlight like a spinnaker, its ground crew ranged around the gondola. The President climbs in, listens to instructions from a thin man in overalls who points to the burner controls. The man backs away. The balloon begins to rise.

The President waves to the onlookers, blows kisses to his family, leans out over the ballast bags and calls out to the crowd.

"Don't worry," he says. "Keep your ears open. Keep your eyes peeled. Keep your nose clean."

He is looking directly at me as these instructions trail off and are no longer audible. I watch until the balloon is only a speck in the northeast sky. Then I return to my car. I am not certain if the President was talking to the Secretary or to me—nor am I at all clear about the meaning of the words.

We are outside the city of P., racing down a narrow road lined with scrawny trees. I am driving a black Mercedes to a secret rendezvous, the radio blaring curious music, the tires kicking up stones that bang against the car's underpan. I am driving very fast, smoking a Turkish cigarette. It is close to noon. The President, a gag over his mouth, his arms and legs trussed with clothesline, is in the trunk of the car.

Once inside the city I drive slowly over cobbled streets, streets teeming with men and women in native dress. I reach a marketplace. In the square some people are shooting a film; I count three cameras. Several men, wearing the foreign garments but looking like Americans, are sitting at the edge of the market with beer bottles in their hands. I stop at a curb, not far from an alley too narrow to enter except on foot, and step out of the car. A real foreigner approaches me; he is tall, bearded, has a battered black cap pulled down to his eyes. He bows. I return the bow.

I say: *The moon is new.*

He smiles. *But the stars know the cares of eternity*, he says.

I say: *All light weakens with time.*

He says: *Try to stay out of camera range.* He enters the alley and waits for me. I follow.

"I have the order," I say.

"I have the money," he tells me, and holds up a cloth pouch. "It is in deutsche-marks."

"That's thoughtful."

"He is alive?"

"Yes," I say.

"He is strong?"

"The ordeal of travel may have weakened him."

"Where is he?"

"In the trunk, the boot of the car."

He gives me the pouch of money. "Wait five minutes," says the foreigner. "Then return to your auto, drive out of the city, and do not look back." He leaves the alley.

I wait. After five minutes have passed, I go back to the car. I look into the trunk; it is empty. I get into the car, start the engine, drive off. The cameras are grinding.

We are on the San Clemente shore at sunset.

"There never *were* such sunsets," the President says. "I'll miss them terribly."

"And they'll miss you," I say.

"I wonder," he says after a moment's musing. "Things have a way of settling themselves."

"They do, sir."

"Of course I've packed up all my belongings."

"Yes, sir."

"And sent postcards to everyone I could think of."

"Yes. I remember mailing them, sir."

The President rubs his eyes. When he turns his back on the sun, two Secret Service men duck down behind the shrubbery. The President looks natty; he is wearing a Park Service uniform, the Sam Browne belt freshly saddlesoaped, the wide-brimmed hat tipped jauntily forward. Down at the main gate a car horn sounds.

"Well," the President says, "that's my ride."

He salutes briskly and jogs down the gravel road toward the gate. I will never see him again. A year from now I will hear that he is transferred to Yellowstone. Two years from now I will find a postcard pushed through my mail slot. It reads:

I am the world's happiest man.

We are at an airport in the Midwest. It is a crisp morning in October, a smell of snow in the air, a panorama of flat brown fields sprawling as far as the eye can see. The President's plane has just come to a stop on the terminal apron; the Secret Service is filing down from the rear exit. The forward door of Air Force One pops out and slides open. The President appears. He acknowledges us from the top of the stairway.

The terminal area is mobbed. Counts range as high as thirty thousand, and the people are—as they say—from all walks of life. The press are waving cameras, housewives wave handkerchiefs, political factionists wave signs. When the President descends, he is met by local dignitaries who take his hand and must be persuaded—a protocol officer whispering in their ears—to let go. A military band is playing astonishing melodies. Cheers erupt on every side. Black limousines are nearly submerged under the winter coats of the crowd.

I am at his right hand as the President begins his movement from the aircraft to the limousine waiting to whisk him into the city. "Hello," the President is saying as he struggles forward. "Good morning. You're very kind. I'm delighted to be here."

To me he says: "Help me. Get me into the car, for God's sake."

I step ahead. With my elbows wide I break a path for the President. The crush is incredible; every now and again I am stopped, almost thrown back.

"Excuse us," I say. Then: "Make way here. Look out. Get the hell back, will you? Move aside. *Move.*"

The crowd thickens. It is like a coagulation; our pace is excruciatingly slow. Finally, yards short of the car, I am stopped in my tracks.

"What is it?" says the President.

Before I can answer, the crowd has separated me from the President, and they are upon him. When I squirm around he is hidden from me by the swarm of men and women. The agents assigned to him are helpless; like me, they have been forced to the outside of the circle. All of us are fighting to get back in. Now I see the crowd's hands lifting aloft: the President's coat, his necktie, his shirt; then one shoe and the other, socks, cotton underwear. *Save me!* It is the voice of the President.

"Make way," I scream. "Make way!"

I can hear the President crying out for help, and once, just for an instant, I catch sight of his face, eyes wild, mouth twisted on some new word he cannot utter.

Addison

I

On the first day I put my plan to work, we were hauling a huge GI can heaped with garbage—Addison and I—moving it out of the mess hall and then across the dirty, slippery concrete loading dock where the truck was waiting. It was a heavy business, and both of us were puffing and wheezing—Addison hanging on to his share of the can with both hands squeezed into the handle, trying not to let his arms be pulled straight because then the handle would crush his fingers against the side of the can. And me. I was doing the best I could with *my one good arm*, as I had trained myself to refer to it in my own thoughts. I had the fingers of my right hand hooked under the handle on my side, and I was lifting as hard as I could. My right knee was bent, so I was able to put some of my body into the job, and I felt myself getting twisted against the can, my muscles pulling every which way and my back beginning to hurt. We both hobbled along, dragging the garbage more than lifting it, progressing by fits and starts.

"Get your end up off of the damned floor," Addison said.

"I'm trying." I ground my hip against my side of the can and tried to use my body to raise it.

"Man," Addison wheezed. He staggered with his side of the can and nearly fell. "Will you *lift?*"

"I'm lifting," I said. My back really hurt, and my right ankle felt twisted.

Addison was back on balance. "You could of ruptured me," he gurgled.

I couldn't say anything. Together, both graceful as camels, we coaxed and clanked and dragged and carried the big silvery can to the edge of the dock. It was a stupid job. Everything smelled, and the flies were all around us, buzzing like furies and looking fierce and slick-green in the fat Texas sun. Even the footing was impossible. Everywhere you stepped there was filth under your shoe—peelings and squashings of God knew what. I could have vomited on the whole business.

We stopped and the GI can went flat on its bottom. I let go of my handle, and Addison straightened up away from the can, rubbing his hands to get the circulation going again. He scowled at me, his one good eye glaring a hole in me.

"Your ass needs a good chewing," he said. He looked away from me, turning and squinting against the sun toward the gray shack across West Virginia Street where the commanding officer and the first sergeant and the orderly-room personnel and all the rest of them lived. I wondered if he was thinking about turning my name in to the flight chief, or maybe to the squadron NCOIC. I decided he wouldn't.

"Everybody should mind his own ass," I said.

Addison kicked the side of the can and pretended to study a piece of potato peel stuck on the edge of one of his new brogans. He brushed the shoe along the edge of the dock and shook the peeling free. "Let's get this mother dumped," he said.

The truck, painted richly blue, was heaped half full with refuse from other mess halls. The driver hadn't bothered to lower the tail-gate—I suppose so he wouldn't lose anything he'd already collected —and that meant we were going to have to raise the GI can up over the edge of the gate before we could dump its contents into the truck. Besides that, the truck was parked at a slight angle to the dock; the corner of the box was up against the dock on my side, but its back edge ran away from the platform so that Addison's corner of the truck was more than two feet out. I should have known then what was likely to happen—and, in fact, I very nearly said something to the driver, who was leaning against a rear wheel chatting with Corporal Harsh.

By this time Addison had already taken hold of his handle—both hands jammed into it, and his jaw set, and his shoulders hunched so I knew he was ready to get the business over with. I liked Addison; you had to get used to his glass eye, because it gave you an eerie feeling of facing some biblical prophet, but after a while you learned to focus on the real eyeball so that conversations with the man made sense. I even got the idea that perhaps he could see better—farther, or deeper—with his one eye than most other men could with two.

I took a one-handed grip on my handle, and nodded to Addison. "Okay," I said.

"Let's us all pull together," Addison said, as if he was leading a tug-of-war team. "Bring her up on three."

I nodded. I could feel the muscles in the backs of my legs get tense, and I squeezed my shoulders forward in imitation of Addison while I waited for the count.

"One," said Addison, "two, *heave!*"

Addison rose up. In the confusion of the moment his bulk turned into a great black silhouette with the sun beyond him, and in the next instant he was gone and I was staring at remote sky. I had expected a different timing. "One, two, three, *go!*" or something like that—the sort of thing little children say before they go off the diving board into the pool, or just at the start of a grade-school foot race. I felt the can all but ripped out of my hand and the lip of it hitting my forearm. I had to let go, and the can dropped back. Addison disappeared. The next thing I knew, I was watching him flounder over the edge of the loading dock, where he hung for a split second with the GI can wobbling on his right foot, and then he went twisting down between the truck bed and the dock to land flat on his face. He let out a horrible shriek—a hair-raising noise such as I have never heard before—and the can clanked once against the tailgate, then toppled over on its side. It caught with a crunch in the space between the truck and the dock, spewing out peels and papers and fruit rinds like a rotten cornucopia. After that, silence. The whole muddle was begun and finished in three or four seconds, and there I was staring down at Addison in a heap under the truck.

While I was looking, I heard someone on the dock behind me. I knew it was the flight chief, Corporal Harsh.

"What's *this* all about?" he said.

"It's Addison," I said. It was a stupid answer, because you could see that everything was about Addison, passed out on the ground, but I couldn't think of anything else.

"What the hell happened?" I watched the corporal limp to the edge of the platform and peer over at the man below. "What's the matter with him?"

Addison's leg looked, to me, as if it was bent the wrong way. "I think he's broken his leg," I said.

"That's great," Corporal Harsh said—perhaps meaning that it was not. He shook his head, angry and unbelieving and in all burdened by Addison.

"I don't actually know how it happened," I started to say.

The corporal took a couple of steps back toward me, and he pointed a finger at me, aiming it between my eyes as though it was a pistol. "I know," he said. "I saw the whole bastardly thing."

"Yes, sir," I said. I looked around to see if there was going to be a crowd listening to me take my chewing-out. There was. A couple of the cooks had come out of the kitchen, wearing their floppy hats, chewing gum, working their big, beefy hands in and around the hems of the dirty-white aprons like a pair of sweaty midwives. Behind them, four or five of the other guys in my flight were gawking into the light, squinty-eyed, those sluggish minds of theirs still back inside the pots and pans they'd been scouring. I had a peach of an audience. I turned my back on them and glanced down at Addison, still stone cold under a little cairn of grapefruit rinds.

"Tell me something, dipshit," Corporal Harsh was saying, "How's it come you throw garbage cans around with one hand?"

"I was doing my best," I said, and I was telling the truth.

"Two hands are better than one." he said.

I agreed with him by nodding.

"Open your mouth," the corporal said. "I can't hear your frigging head rattle."

"Yes, sir."

Corporal Harsh shook his own head slowly, the way you would if you were dealing with a five-year-old who'd broken a toy you'd just given him. "Collins, by damn, you are a royal pain to me in this flight."

"I'm sorry, sir," I said.

"Of all the dipshits, you are number one."

"Yes, sir."

"Next time, use both hands. Garbage is heavy. Your buddy Addison didn't hardly have a chance the way you let down on your end. Okay? Two hands from now on." He started to turn away from me and go off toward the kitchen. I followed and stopped him just as he was about to get out of the sun. The screen doors into the mess were still wide open, stuck against the walls by the weight of cooks and KP's who were my witness, and whole escadrilles of flies zoomed in and out of the mess hall.

"Sir?" I said. "Corporal Harsh, sir?"

He stopped and rested his fists on his hips. "Do me a frigging favor, Collins. Get back on that garbage detail, and do it *right now*." He surveyed the dull faces looming in the doorway. "Clay," he said, "give Collins a hand."

"Sir, I just can't do it. I can't lift that can of garbage." It made me feel inadequate to say it, and even a little ashamed, but it had to be said. "Honestly, sir. I don't want to hurt anybody else."

The corporal studied me without much sign of comprehending me. "What the hell is the matter, Collins?"

"I only have one arm, sir."

His mouth opened, then closed, and I could hear the fat flies zooming in and out of the kitchen behind him. He made a great production out of me; first he touched my right hand.

"That's one," he said. "Is that right, airman?"

"Yes, sir."

Then he touched my left hand. "And that's two. Is that also right?" He cocked his head to one side; he had on the soft o.d. fatigue cap, heavily starched, with the crown painstakingly flattened on top in imitation of the hard caps I had seen the army wear. I had long since decided I was going to wear my cap—when they gave me one—squared off like his.

"One, two," Harsh repeated. "Now what was the problem, airman?"

"I'm sorry, sir, but I can't use my left arm."

"Why the hell not?"

"I don't know. I don't have any control over it."

"*Sir,*" he said.

"Yes, sir. I don't, sir."

Corporal Harsh circled me unevenly. "What's the gag, Collins? Has your arm gone to sleep?"

"No, sir."

"Did you hurt it on something? Slam it in your footlocker? Somebody step on it in the shower?"

I shook my head before I remembered that the corporal couldn't hear it rattle. "No, sir. I simply don't have any feeling there. No sensation at all."

Corporal Harsh was in front of me again, looking dimly worried. Everybody was staring at me and there were more and more flies.

"Well, God damn it, do you mean to stand there and ask me to believe that your frigging arm is just *hanging* from your shoulder like a skinny soupbone?"

"Yes, sir."

Corporal Harsh scratched the end of his nose and cast a sidewise look at one of the cooks bundling and unbundling his greasy apron nearby. "Now isn't that a wild one?" he said.

The cook looked wise and nodded gravely, still chewing his cud of gum. "Beats the crap out of me," the cook said.

The corporal returned to me. "We're going to try a little experiment," he said. "A funny game."

"Yes, sir," I said.

"I want you to turn your head away—off to the right so you can't see me standing on this side of you. Got it?"

"Like he was checking you for hernia," the cook added.

I turned my head to show that I understood. I found myself

looking squarely into the face of Woodrow Clay, a jaundice-eyed young man from McAllen, Texas, whose bunk was above mine in the barracks. It was a grinning face, eager for God knew what.

"And I'm going to poke your arm and ask you to tell me how many fingers," Corporal Harsh said. "Got that?"

"Yes, sir." I waited.

"How many?" he asked. I stared blankly into Clay's yellow eyes. Clay looked around, feverish, then spastically lifted two fingers to scratch his left ear.

I said: "I can't tell, sir." Clay looked hurt and took his fingers out of his ear.

"You mean you can't count, either?"

"I didn't feel anything, sir."

"Nothing?"

"No, sir." Clay winked at me. The rest of the audience set up a chorus of mumbling that drowned out the flies.

"How about now?" Harsh said. Clay had taken his cue from somebody I couldn't see, and now he was plucking imbecilely at his lower lip with four fingers.

"No, sir." I felt the corporal walking around to where he could face me. "Nothing, sir," I repeated. Clay was chewing his fingernails behind the corporal.

"Dipshit," Corporal Harsh said, "if you are trying to screw off of KP, your ass is grass."

"Yes, sir."

"Why didn't you tell me about this frigging arm of yours before now?"

"I thought I could get by with it," I said.

"Who asked you to think, airman?"

I couldn't come up with an answer. Corporal Harsh shielded his eyes with his hand; even in shadow, his eyes were slits when he looked at me. "You're a real clown, aren't you, Collins?" he said venomously.

"Not intentionally, sir." I wished he would move away from the right of me, so I could stop feeling like a tableau from the Great Seal.

The corporal turned abruptly to face the others who were still hanging around the dock. "All you guys don't like to take shots, get Collins to stand in line for you," he said. "His arm's so dead, it stinks." Everybody laughed, and Corporal Harsh gave his attention back to me. "That okay by you, airman?"

"It's all right, sir."

"How long you been in the air force, Collins?"

"Two weeks, sir."

"Do you mind if I ask how you got past the frigging physical with one frigging arm?"

"I don't know, sir."

"Did they *give* you a physical?"

"Yes, sir. They did."

"What were the doctors? Blind drunk?"

"I don't think so, sir." I finally turned my head forward to get the stiffness out of my neck. Corporal Harsh roamed in front of me. "I guess they were busy, sir."

"I should guess to hell they were," he said. He turned on the crowd. "Clay, get on that frigging garbage detail," he ordered, "and you, Morrison, you help him. The rest of your screws-offs get back inside for chow. *Right now!*"

Everybody scattered. Except for Clay and Morrison, who were indifferently committed to righting Addison's and my GI can at the end of the platform, only Corporal Harsh and I were left on the dock.

"You want me to go in for chow, sir?" I asked.

He scowled at me. "I want you to wait, airman. I want you to cool your frigging heels on an empty gut until every last flight in the thirty-seven-oh-fourth has gone through the line. *Then* you eat the scraps. You got that?"

"Yes, sir."

The corporal went unevenly to the end of the dock and looked over the edge. "Morrison," he said without turning to the man, "get this nigger an ambulance."

"Right, sir." Morrison let go of the garbage can and ran into the mess hall like a man prancing on smashed glass. The can fell over again in galvanized clamor. Corporal Harsh twitched at the noise; Clay swore; I stood, not knowing what to do.

The corporal came back to me. "Collins, I'm not finished with you by a frigging long shot."

"No, sir."

"You come up to my quarters at nineteen-thirty hours, sharp. I'm going to get the straight skinny out of you if I have to boot your tail from here to Dallas and back."

"Yes, sir."

"Now take off." He started to leave me.

"What should I do until the rest of them are through eating?" I asked him.

For a moment he seemed uncertain. He looked at Clay, who was lighting a cigarette next to the toppled GI can, then he looked at my left hand, and then he looked at me. "You take your wise ass across the street and start policing the area in front of the headquarters building," he said. "You do that until I tell you it's time for chow. All right?"

"Yes, sir."

"Any time I look out a window, all I want to see of you is ass and elbows. Now get to it." He went through the screen doors into the mess hall, brushing flies from his face all the way.

There was a row of seven or eight garbage cans along the wall of the mess, and I went over to the end of the row to pick up my sport coat and tie. Clay met me there, grinning. His teeth were marvelously green; if you were a dentist, you could have made your career out of Woodrow Clay's mouth.

"You want a cigarette?" Clay said.

I shook my head and flung the coat over my shoulder, getting ready to go and police the area across the street.

"I thought I seen you smoking."

"Sometimes."

"Meaning you don't feel like smoking just now?"

"Not right this minute." I started to leave him. I had no quarrel with Clay, and I didn't dislike him, but I had the vague notion that the two of us had nothing to talk about. Besides, since the first intrusion of the world into my waking every morning consisted of Woodrow Clay's grimy feet dangling before my eyes—and the second was the uncanny vision of his stark, scrawny buttocks plummeting like a broken meteor across my sight as he dropped to the floor—I felt we already shared intimacies enough.

"You got old Harsh shaking the bees out of his head," Clay said. "He don't know what to do on your account."

"Is that so?"

"What I only wanted to ask you was: How come you didn't catch on to my signals and tell him how many fingers? Billy Joe Miller was next to him, and he was giving me the right answers."

"Why should I give the right answers if I couldn't feel anything?" I asked.

"No lie? You couldn't feel nothing?"

"Nothing."

"Hell, Yankee," and Clay's face lit up with something like admiration, "they'll give you a goddam discharge right smack out of the air force. You hopped up smelling like a rose."

"Thanks," I said. I shuffled my feet in a small pile of coffee grounds.

"That's a swell-looking jacket you got," Clay said.

"It used to be," I said.

"I'm partial to blue," Clay said.

"Me too." I'd have given a lot to be able to say something flattering about Clay's taste in clothes, but since we were all still wearing the civilian outfits we had enlisted in, and since it had been two weeks and there had been no time to have the clothes on our backs cleaned or washed, no one of us in the flight was a men's-magazine picture. Clay was wearing Levi's and a soiled undershirt; I wouldn't for a moment have criticized his clothes—my own gabardine slacks were baggy and streaked with dust and three-corner torn, and my white shirt was the next thing to maggoty—but I couldn't admire them. It must have been a kind of desperation that led Clay to say nice words about my sport coat, which—I noticed when I tossed it over my shoulder—was turning vaguely yellow down in the narrow valleys of the corduroy.

"Well," I said, shrugging my good shoulder, "I've got to go out and clean up the area." I turned around.

"That was pretty good," Clay said to my back. "What you did to that nigra."

"I didn't do it on purpose."

"But it was pretty good."

I crossed the platform and jumped to the ground, trying to be cat-like and resilient, but landing hard enough to jar my teeth down to the backs of my knees. The truck driver was squatted beside Addison, who hadn't moved, saying: "C'mon, old buddy, let's wake up now. Let's rise and shine, old buddy," and waddling awkwardly around the unconscious man, picking off eggshells and fruit rinds one at a time and pumping them up into the great mouth of the GI can over his head.

I started across West Virginia Street into a sun which was high enough to be tropically hot. It was January, and days which began before dawn with temperatures in the twenties blew up into afternoons in the nineties. The asphalt pavement was soft under my new brogans—the first installment on our military issue—and it felt as if I was leaving footprints. I heard Clay call after me: "Hey, Yankee, you want to take my flu shot for me?" I turned, still walking, and improvised a broad, false smile.

In front of the squadron headquarters was a white mailbox on a white post, set at the corner where the narrow graveled walk met the paved street. I hung my coat over it, stuffed my necktie into a pocket, and began roaming, half-bent, looking for things to police up. What I was after, mostly, was cigarette butts and gum wrappers. It was slim pickings here, now, and I suspected that earlier in the day a whole flight of seventy men—perhaps a half-dozen flights—had scoured this area and deprived me.

I ranged over a relatively narrow field, bounded on one side by the headquarters building, and on the other three by a row of round stones painstakingly whitewashed. Lackland Air Force Base was studded with millions of round, whitewashed stones. It was stagger-ing to try and imagine all of them—like trying to imagine the num-ber of grains of sand on a beach—or all the young Americans armed with buckets and brushes, who had been recruited through the years to whiten and rewhiten them. If war had no other meanings, the splendor of these rocks would have seemed nearly worth the dying.

At any rate, I ranged the area diligently, sometimes simian, sometimes fully erect. In an odd way I was both pleased and irritated to find a cigarette butt before me. It was a justification of myself—an affirmation of soldierliness—to catch hold of some real *thing* and tuck it into the pocket of my trousers. At the same time, it was annoying to think that there were men on this reservation who didn't know how to field-strip a cigarette. I saw something neat, *correct*, in letting loose tobacco vanish on the winds, and letting the earth take the infinitely small pill of wadded paper that remained. Among my other exercises of the past two weeks—ever since I had dropped out of college and enlisted to subvert the draft—I had practiced field-stripping my cigarettes with elaborate patience, until I was able to do it with one hand as naturally as other men with two.

But during the hour of my policing stint I deliberately did not field-strip the four cigarettes I smoked, so as to give myself work to do. And I found two gum wrappers—one, actually, but both the inner and outer papers. Nothing else turned up. I memorized each bare, brown patch in the withered gray lawn; I counted the white-washed stones—seventy-seven; I looked in at the windows of the headquarters building and saw desks and typewriters and young men in tieless khaki uniforms exchanging handfuls of papers, and on a long bench near the front door two or three recruits in fatigue suits who were waiting to become messengers.

Eventually Corporal Harsh came limping across West Virginia Street to interrupt my reveries.

"Straighten up, dipshit," he said. "Get some chow."

I retrieved my coat and tie from the squadron mailbox and followed the corporal back to the mess hall. I noticed that the garbage truck was still parked at the end of the dock, and I saw that an ambulance had at last come for Addison. A pair of medics was heaping him on a stretcher; they slid him into the boxy dark of the ambulance and whisked him away in a northerly direction—possibly to a hospital.

I truly wanted Addison to be made whole. My arm and I had already caused trouble enough, or so I thought—too green to realize then that the military has ways of compounding the difficulties a man thinks he has learned to bear with. That there was nothing wrong with my left arm, Corporal Harsh must have guessed at once; he must have known that no battery of doctors and psychologists, however lax, could have let a one-armed man slide through the air force physical. He might have thought that if I had been telling the truth about my handicap, then the arm should have been withered and repulsive. Something. I don't know what, but some outward sign of its deadness; perhaps an odd cast to the color of the skin, or a special gauntness under the flesh. Clearly, Harsh was wise to me. If you close your eyes and try to count the pressure of one, two, three fingers against your arm, you find the task impossible. Harsh knew that his "test" was no test; only Woodrow Clay didn't know. Yet if I was stupidly determined to play my deception out to the end, so, apparently, was my flight chief.

II

Now, looking back, I understand that none of it *needed* to happen —that it was entirely a matter of the exercise of some sort of subversive moral sensibility, perhaps an act of will and nothing purely or simply else. So—I see clearly—there can be no question of blaming Addison, or Corporal Harsh, or the men I served with, or even the doctors who took part in the grotesque final act I never witnessed. No one is at fault; only me. Only I.

It was, in a way, good discipline for me. It was never the kind of discipline the air force could have understood, for the military's concern is with the manipulation of numbers rather than ciphers. You will see that; the crisis resulted inevitably from the conflict between my discipline and theirs, and it was Corporal Harsh who made the conflict plain.

At 1930 hours, sharp, it was Acting Corporal Leery who let me into Corporal Harsh's quarters on the second floor of the barracks. I heard the door close in back of me. I saw Corporal Harsh sprawled in a corner of the room in an old leather armchair. The only sounds were the distant shouts of my barracks-mates, who were involved in a GI party and were already in the midst of sloshing big buckets of water over the wooden floors outside the closed door.

I raised my good arm in a proper salute. "Sir," I chanted, "Airman Basic Collins, Robert F., AF 18380568, reporting as ordered, sir." I wasn't sure if the phrase lacked balance, or had too much.

Corporal Harsh touched his brow and dropped his hand into his lap. He was wearing his undershirt, and his fatigue trousers were half unbuttoned. For several seconds—it seemed longer—he said nothing; he only looked at me, my face, my shoes, my left arm.

Finally he said: "Airman Collins." He said it without any expression, as if he was memorizing it. "Airman Collins. Just one more wise-ass from Texas, is that it?" He tipped his head and studied me.

"No, sir," I said.

"No what?"

"I'm not from Texas, sir."

We all floated in another long silence while Corporal Harsh considered what I had said.

"Leery?" the corporal said.

"Yeah?" I heard Leery's feet shuffling behind me.

"You go on out there and make sure there's enough brushes and laundry soap. Get everybody on the stick."

"Right." The door opened and closed.

Corporal Harsh found himself a cigarette and lit it. "Now what the hell, airman?" he said. "What's that serial number of yours?"

"Sir, it's AF 18380568." I saluted again.

"Put your hand down. It's just a frigging number, not the flag."

"Yes, sir."

The corporal breathed smoke. "Now damn it, Collins, that serial number says you're from Texas, doesn't it?"

"I was working in Texas when I enlisted, sir."

"Where *are* you from?"

"The State of Maine, sir."

"Maine," he echoed.

"Yes, sir."

A third silence. I looked down at my feet to see if the angle between my shoes was 45 degrees. "You're at attention, airman," Corporal Harsh said, and I looked up.

The fourth silence. Then the corporal began again.

"Just one more wise-ass from Maine, is that it?" he said.

"I don't know, sir."

"What the hell does that mean?"

"I don't think I'm trying to be wise, sir."

"Well I think you are."

"Yes, sir."

The corporal settled, if anything, deeper into the cracked leather
of his chair and stroked the back of his head with the hand that held
the smoldering cigarette. His other hand—the right—made scratching motions across the exposed triangle of undershorts and belly
showing at the top of his fatigue pants.

"Tell me again about the arm, do you mind?"

"Just that I can't use it, sir."

"You can't use it at all, is that right?"

"No, sir."

"No, that *isn't* right?"

"No, I can't use it at all. Sir."

Corporal Harsh stared at me and smoked. Standing rigidly before
him in my yellowed blue coat and my civilian shirt and slacks—held
up, it seemed to me, only by the high tops of my issue brogans—I began to feel the heat of the room. Absorbing all day the uncomprom-
ising rays of the Texas sun, the barracks after dark were like ovens,
and the air in them turgid with humidity and high temperature. I
noticed sweat trickling slow and cool under my arms and down my
sides; I hoped Corporal Harsh might put me at ease—that he might
even suggest that I take off my coat.

"And how long have you had this—this infirmity?" It seemed a
word—"infirmity"—the corporal rarely used.

"Since before I enlisted, sir."

He nodded slowly. "You are an enlistee?"

"Yes, sir."

"Why did you enlist, if you don't mind me asking?"

"I was 1-A, sir."

Corporal Harsh raised an eyebrow. "You enlisted to beat the draft?"

"Something like that. I joined the air force to avoid the infantry, sir."

Harsh looked about to laugh. He didn't; instead he said: "Collins, you are either an asshole, or time means nothing to you."

"Time means nothing to me, sir." I was a little pleased to have been given the choice.

"It won't get you out," the corporal said. He dropped the cigarette onto the floor in front of him and squashed it out with one unlaced boot.

"Sir?"

"Having one arm won't get you out. No medical discharge. Not even a section eight, if you're a nut—which I think you are."

"I don't want to get out, sir." And that was the truth, even then.

"You see, Collins," and here he leaned forward and pulled up one leg of his fatigues, "I've only got one leg."

"Yes, sir. I know."

As a matter of fact, I had known Corporal Harsh was a cripple from the first day of my arrival at Lackland. I had figured it out from the curious way he paced as he lectured all of us on the part he was to play in our military lives—serving in the stead of all the loved ones we had known as civilians, but not including our girlfriends lest we be tempted to screw him—and from the one-legged manner of his standing still, and from noticing the fact that he could *count* cadence but could not march to it. But this was the first time I had actually *seen* the artificial leg—an odd conglomeration of rods and straps attached, I assumed, to his real leg at or just below the knee. I felt a smallish shock at the sight; I guess I had expected something of wood, some construction of cork, as in pirate movies.

"Then we have something in common, don't we, airman?"

"We do, sir."

Corporal Harsh dropped the pantleg. "Only not as much as you'd maybe like to think," he went on. "Because there's a big difference between us, too. It's the difference between an arm and a leg, right?"

"Of course, sir."

"And a little bit more than that." He lit another cigarette and slumped back in the armchair. "It's a real funny difference, Airman Collins. See if *you* don't think it's real funny. You've got your arm, and it's all there for the world to see, but you can't feel anything. I got no leg at all from the joint down, but I can feel *everything*. I can feel my toes, but I got no toes. I can feel an itch on my foot, but I can't scratch it because I got no foot. Can you imagine that?"

"No, sir, I can't," I said.

"You're goddamned right, you can't!" Harsh yelled the words at me, and his face was suddenly red. "You stupid dipshit, you can't even dream the kind of hell I go through!"

There came a knocking at the door.

"Who the hell is it?"

"Corporal Leery. You all right, Ken?"

"Buzz off, Leery. I'll call you if I need you."

I stood quietly, still at attention, while Corporal Harsh slouched in the chair before me. He took deep breaths, scowling at the cigarette in his hand, and when he seemed to have re-collected himself he rubbed at the sweat on his forehead with his free hand.

"At ease, airman." The order came almost as a sigh. I put my left foot away from me, and slid my right arm behind my back while the corporal watched me narrowly. Since I had never begun practicing parade rest with both arms, I didn't even have to think to leave my left arm loose at my side.

Harsh studied me. Finally he said: "Tell me something, Collins. How do you dress?"

"Sir?"

"How do you get your clothes on and off, with just one arm? I think it would be damned hard to manage."

"Sometimes it is, sir. Sometimes you have to make use of things that are around you; once in a while I have to push against things—a piece of furniture, or a post or something—to sort of scrape the clothes off myself. I guess it looks funny."

"Why don't you show me, Collins."

"Show you, sir?"

"Yes; show me. Show me how you'd take off that rancid coat you're wearing."

"That's fairly easy, sir. You just pull it off your shoulder from the bottom, and then you shrug yourself out of it. After that, you lean—and the coat slides down the bad arm." I was showing him as I talked; the blue coat lay in a heap beside me. "In general," I said, "any piece of clothing that opens up the center is no problem."

Corporal Harsh pursed his mouth and nodded. "That's damned interesting," he said. "You do the same thing with that shirt you got on?"

"Yes, sir. Just unbutton it and work it off the shoulder from the shirttail end."

"Could I see it again?"

"Sir?" I realized what was happening.

"Take off the shirt, airman. That's an order."

In a matter of ten minutes or so Corporal Harsh had me standing naked in front of him—having forced me to show him the whole repertoire of my one-armed undressing talents, while he himself sat smoking and listening to my commentary and, once in a while, interrupting with a question. He wanted to know, for example, why I wore no undershirt, and nodded wisely as I explained the considerable difficulty posed by clothing which had neither buttons nor zippers nor any medial opening of size—how a man ought properly to be double-jointed if he wished to extricate his good arm without tearing the garment. I pointed out that getting an undershirt *on* was quite a simple task; and then I was half afraid he would ask me to demonstrate with a borrowed shirt—that he would laugh to see me struggling to remove it after I had put it on. He was curious how I dealt with shoes—whether I had to sit down to take them off, or whether I could keep my balance on one foot even though I had no free arm to steady myself. I showed him that I could keep my balance, both for shoes and socks, and he pretended to be impressed.

After I had taken off my trousers—easiest of all—I hoped the corporal would end the entertainment. It was no surprise that he made me go on until all my clothes lay in a heap around me; he was, after all, punishing me—both for what I had done to Addison, and for the way I had undermined his discipline in our dialogue on the loading dock of the mess hall. I could not resent the way he chose to humiliate me—though I had not imagined how far he was to carry the humiliation—and throughout my performance in front of him Corporal Harsh was in no way vicious or cruel. I think he took no special pleasure from my nakedness—there was no shadow of perversion in his commands, nothing of the universal smirking homosexuality which flavors the gossip of every military situation. Simply, he was getting even with me on my own terms—by testing the incredible story I had recited to him after the incident with Addison. While later on I would not have done so, at this time I admired Corporal Harsh's grasp of human psychology, for as he tested and punished me he was simultaneously permitting me to show off the thoroughness of my plan. Thus we were both benefiting.

Now that I was stripped, the atmosphere of the room changed abruptly. The corporal stood up; he fastened the belt and buttons of his fatigues and walked a wide circle around me. He stopped in front of me. It was as if we were back on the loading dock, and Addison still unconscious over the edge.

"Come to attention, dipshit," Harsh said.

I obeyed.

"Now I want twenty-five pushups. Move!"

It is difficult to do pushups with one arm; still, I had practiced diligently during two weeks of morning drill, and I dropped to the floor without hesitation—my right arm under my chest in such a way that at the top of the exercise my weight would be more or less centered over it. The corporal counted for me, and as he counted, he circled to the door of his room and pulled it wide open.

The rest of the flight was still in the midst of the GI party, the sounds of buckets and water and brushes filling the small room around my exertions, and the smell of damp wood and yellow soap mingling—in my own nostrils, at least—with the odor of sweat. By the time Corporal Harsh had counted to ten, the noise of objects had begun to diminish, replaced by a rising volume of human voices. Then the voices died out, so that as I puffed and gasped through the twenties of my pushups there were no other sounds than the jingle of my dogtags against the floor and the cadence set by Corporal Harsh.

"Get all the way down, Collins," said a voice that was probably Leery's. "Let's see a few splinters in those nuts of yours."

I did not cheat. I did go all the way down, so that my chest touched the back of my hand, and I did come all the way up, so that the chain around my neck swung free under me. When I had fulfilled my assignment, the corporal allowed me to rest—prone, the blood pounding behind my eyes, the floor cool and hard along the length of my body. In the doorway the feet of my comrades—some bare, some booted—occupied the blur of my vision.

"What'd he do, sir?" Woodrow Clay's voice, eternally nasal and incredulous.

"He's qualifying," Corporal Harsh said. "He's qualifying himself to be a one-armed fighting machine." He nudged my side with his artificial foot. "On your feet, Collins."

I got up and stood at attention, facing the door. Uncountable heads filled the opening—wide eyed, wide mouthed.

"All right," Harsh said grimly. "Fall in for inspection. Right now. *On the double!*" The amazed faces fell away from the door; Woodrow Clay, Billy Joe Miller, a score of men whose names I never learned—all of them tumbled back through the barracks to take positions in a double line before their bunks. From my vantage point I could see the absurdity of this inspection, the men in various stages of undress, the floor half-wet, half-dry, a chaos of buckets and soap cakes and stiff brushes littering the aisle between the two ranks. Beds were unmade; the toes of socks and sleeves of grimy civilian clothes kept locker lids from closing. Here was a marvel of disorder.

"March," the corporal told me. He halted me just inside the barracks proper, and then he made a brief speech. He told the thirty-five men drawn up at attention that they all knew me, and how they likewise knew I had no sensation in my left arm. He said he appreciated my handicap, as he was himself minus a limb. Nevertheless, he reminded them, my failure to report myself and my handicap to a proper authority had led to an unfortunate accident involving one Henry Addison—for which breach of military behavior I deserved to be punished. Since no one wishes to do harm to a cripple,

Harsh said, it occurred to him that the appropriate justice for my case consisted in directing punishment against that part of me which was already insensate—thus making my crime clear to me without causing me unnecessary pain.

In conclusion, Corporal Harsh doubled his fist and struck my left arm—hard—just below the shoulder, then ordered me to walk the length of the barracks and back between the double row of my fellows.

It was so eloquent an address, and the punctuation of that first blow on the arm so *right*, that the first man in line on my left never lifted his hand to me. The second man did, but he was Woodrow Clay and he pulled his punch. From the third man on, however, no one omitted to strike me and no one was gentle. All of them believed my story.

It isn't easy to explain how a man goes about crippling himself. Concentration, surely. I needn't say more about my first two weeks as a recruit than that it had been necessary for me to focus all my sensibilities for most of my waking hours—not *on* my left arm, for I think that would have been easier, but away from it, pretending to myself that it did not exist, that it had never existed, that I had no use for it whatever. And practice. All that other men did with two hands, I taught myself to do with one, and every day brought a new task—one I had not thought of—to be rehearsed and added to the range of my abilities. I had never realized—to name a small thing— that I used both hands in the act of shaving, one hand to stretch the skin under the blade; imagine the facial contortions I had to become accustomed to! Or lacing shoes with one hand; tying a necktie; merely writing a letter. I had begun to fancy myself quite an artist.

Certainly I had known premonitions of pain—had known the time of testing would come. Against it, I had done my best. I had cultivated a stoicism I gauged when I was alone by pinching my bad arm, pricking it with whatever sharp object was available—at first with my teeth gritted and scarcely able to restrain a cry or a curse, but eventually without a tremor. It was as if, after a few days of self-torture, I had traumatized the arm; I found that I felt nothing unless I wished to feel. But I never deluded myself; I never pretended that there was not greater pain in the world than I could invent for myself; I always conceded that the weapon I used on myself would be more brutally wielded in the hands of another. What reflex scream might answer a scalding, a burning, a deeper laceration—I could not predict, and now, put upon by my fellow recruits, I quickly found how little I was in control of my own pretense.

Yet I was not found out. What saved me was the animal eagerness of my mates, for as I stumbled up and down the line of clenched fists and took blow after blow from them, those standing on my right became too excited to wait for their proper turn in the entertainment. Impatient and excited—and unaccountably enraged against me— the men swung at me from both sides, and the force of their punches, the randomness of them, the viciousness with which they spun me around, these made it possible for me to shout the hurt I felt. For all anyone knew, I cried out only when my good arm was struck, but in fact I was learning for the first time that all of my self-teaching had gone for nothing. Both arms ached, both arms burst from pain, both arms taught me the pitifully low threshold of my nervous system. Miraculously, I was hurt nowhere else. Except for the occasional accidental weight of someone's brogan on my bare feet as I was spun up and down the line, no one struck any part of me but my arms—my left mercilessly, my right less severely.

How long the punishment lasted, I can't say. What I remember in retrospect had no dimension in time; the event measures itself strictly in space and noise and changes of light. Fists rose and fell like sequences of hammers inside a piano, shouts filled my ears, the overhead lightbulbs flashed in and out of my field of vision like a mad Ferris wheel. Through it all the pain drummed like engines made to run faster and faster. The last thing I remember is falling like a rag animal to the floor—feeling the wet floor against my buttocks, seeing the bruises on my poor arm, hearing a noise triumphant as a cheer. I lay over someone's footlocker—perhaps my own—and fainted. Briefly, three or four times, I came to my senses; I saw myself inside a circle, saw the blade of a knife; I remember blood I knew was mine, and laughter that may have been mine. The last words over me:

"Maybe it's paralyzed, but it sure bleeds okay."

I don't know who said it. Perhaps Woodrow Clay—the words were so incredulous.

III

I awoke in a narrow bed surrounded by other beds whose pale outlines I was only dreamily aware of. I came to my senses slowly—later, the doctors were to tell me that I had been under their care for nearly four days—floating up out of a strange mixture of real and imagined circumstances. At one point I was across the street from the squadron mess hall, dressed in my rotten civilian clothes, standing straight as a post. All around me was a panorama of the 3704th Training Squadron—a bustle of men and voices that was phenomenal even in hallucination. At the front of the mess hall arrived flight after flight of young men, marched there by chronically angry corporals, halted and made to stand at parade rest, in formation. A dismal sunlight gargled over them, spitting their shadows onto the steaming asphalt and down the graveled gullies beside the roads; they stood sweating, raggedly in line, staring at the ground. One column at a time they jerked to attention and marched single file to the door of the mess, stopped, rested, trickled inside until the long white building had gulped in the last of them. Then the next column unshuffled itself. It was a nightmare of eternity.

When they came out from the rear of the building, the recruits emerged by twos and threes—talking and lighting cigarettes, punching and scuffling at each other like children; I heard their laughter, but not the sense of their words. They crossed a loading dock identical to the one where Corporal Harsh had first tested me for truth, and they jumped down in slow motion, never so much as losing their caps. On the sick grass they gathered in clusters of four and five, smoked, waited. Some sat on the starved lawn; others lay on their bellies and leaned on their elbows and stared through the flumes of their cigarettes toward the blocked sky; still others sprawled indolently on their backs, with their fingers locked across their chests and their soft caps tilted over their eyes. After a while a flight chief came out; he mounted the dusty shoulder to the street, collected his nameless charges in a column of fives, and hupped them out of sight.

And then I was one of them, one of the eternal flights of recruits, marching in my usual place—second man of the left outside file. Corporal Harsh limped to my left, counting and counting, watching us narrowly. In front of me was Addison, taller than I and a superb marcher, everything about his body graceful and perfectly under control. I envied him—even in this curious dream—as you might envy a dancer whose movements were inevitably beautiful. The corporal screamed in my ear: "Who's that bouncing? Collins, stop bouncing up and down! You march like you got a cob up, Collins. Collins! Collins!" And there was nothing I could do but bounce and grit my teeth, and try to let my arms swing naturally, and do my best to move my legs from the hips and nowhere higher. I thought if he hadn't put me so close to Addison, so close to perfection, he would not so easily have noticed how badly I marched.

And finally we were marching straight into an ocean such as Texas will never see again, sloshing forward, ankle deep, knee deep, hip deep, until the cadence broke and we were all swimming for our lives. It was—dear God!—Wells Beach from my childhood, the cold blue water packed with swimmers, and the tide coming in at the end of the afternoon. I had been sitting on an enormous rock a hundred yards from the beach; I had lost track of time, forgotten where I was until the waves began to buffet me; now I was swimming—a bad swimmer, not as good as Addison—trying to get back to the beach, the concrete breakwater, the chain-link fence, the parking lot, the white casino. My arms were so tired with thrashing, I thought they would fall off.

This is the way I retrieved enough of my senses to realize I was in the hospital—by bursting out of the water onto the fringe of white beach, while summer people hovered over me. In fact, they had rescued me; in fact, my arms had fallen off.

What the air force doctors told me made—at the time—about as much sense as the dreams had. They filled me with explanations, reports of medical examinations, recapitulations of worried conferences and difficult decisions. Bones so badly fractured, they said, and muscles torn past repair. You had visions of marrow oozing under a butcher's cleaver, and tendons like spider webs clawed out of the doors of old houses. Blood loss, they said; think of running a mower over a garden hose. Graphic, their descriptions. Both my arms ached; I could feel every bruise, every cut, every thread of lameness down to the tips of my fingers—again, in both my arms. The game was up; the plan exposed. They had saved my right arm, the doctors said, but they had cut away the left in order to salvage my life for me.

I passed out. When I opened my eyes again, still high on whatever narcotic was keeping me sane, I was alone in the white bed. My right arm—*my one good* arm—was in a cast and immobilized against my side; my left arm wasn't even a bulge under the sheet. A huge fist of cloth clenched my bad shoulder. I shrugged, and felt the pain through layer after layer of sedation. Blessedly, I wasn't able to think.

Eventually I realized I wasn't alone in the room. The other beds were occupied, probably by men less willful than myself, and I began to make them out—their heads, all turned toward me, and the hills of their knees under the covers. Then—revelation!—I saw Addison. He was in a bed beside my own, his right leg wrapped in white and held a few inches off the mattress by an arrangement of pulleys and wires. He looked squarely at me; in the half-dark of the ward, his glass eye shone like a gemstone.

"Man," he said, "I hope you are satisfied."

I had no answer for him. If the question had come from Corporal Harsh—even though we shared the knowledge of sensation in the amputated limb—I could not have shaken the balloon of my giddy head in the rattle of an answer. Everything had come true for me, but in a world like this, what is the measure of satisfaction?

The Apple

She thought about the apple all Sunday afternoon and evening, telling herself it was truly thinking—and not daydreaming—that possessed her. She was apprehensive; the apprehension came out in random actions. She did her nails, she smoked, she chose something to wear and in that process rearranged the hangers in the closet. She made decisions: she would not smoke so much; she would not tell her mother about the apple. She changed her mind about a red dress, in favor of a green suit. She dabbed a fingertip against her tongue and tried to rub away a small soiled spot on the toe of one of her white shoes.

Just at sunset, she lay down on the narrow bed drawn close to the window of her room and looked out, leaning on one bare elbow. The last light filtered through the small foliage of the park across the way and played leaves over her face. The street was empty and looked washed. She lit another cigarette and laid it on the window ledge; the tip of it hung over the edge of the sill and its smoke fanned up in a filigree of weak sunlight both yellow and blue.

She lay, smoking one cigarette after another, until the room was dark. She was still thinking about the apple. She was thinking that if she knew his name, then she would introduce him to her mother; not to know it was to make the introduction an embarrassment. She could explain later, when she got home. The street lights were on. She persuaded herself to get up and dress, and while she was naked she heard her mother knock at the door.

"Julie? Are you awake?"

"Yes, Mother."

"It's late. Don't you want something to eat?"

She took a quick, interrupted breath. "I'm going out, Mother; no, thank you."

She heard her mother moving on the other side of the door. "Julie? Are you lying there in the dark?"

"Not now. I just this minute got up to dress."

"Don't make yourself ill, dear."

Her mother went away. Julie turned on the dresser lamp and puttered among the objects arranged on the glass top: cosmetics and scents, a picture of her late father, a framed snapshot of herself when she was five.

As she dressed, she realized how silly her fears were. How could she fret about introducing him to her mother? He would surely not come to the door for her; how did she imagine he would get up the porch steps? *Bump, bump, bump.* That *would* have disturbed her mother. She finished dressing, making her face; she gave up on the blemished shoe.

At nine o'clock she went to the window. It was the time agreed upon, and though she had not heard a car, she was not surprised to look down to the curb and see her own convertible—green, but looking black under the dim street-bulbs—waiting in front of the house. And there was the nameless apple seated in front on the passenger side, punctual and expecting her. She took up her purse and hurried downstairs.

At the foot of the staircase her mother hindered her.

"Is that the boy outside? Wouldn't he like to come in?"

Julie kissed her mother's cheek. "'Bye," she said. "I'll tell you everything when I get home." She pushed open the front door and half-ran across the porch, her heels hollow in the quiet street.

No one else was in sight. She crossed in front of the car and got in behind the wheel. She smiled at the apple; he was sitting beside her, nestled against the door. In the weak light he seemed somehow melancholy, with the world reflected from his skin like an image in a thick lens. In her own mind she had formed a picture of him as she lay upstairs on her bed. In the picture, light had shone from him as through a small, curved window—the way she had always drawn him. Here, in fact, the window blurred.

"I hope you haven't been waiting long," she said. "I almost forgot the time."

He didn't answer; she hadn't expected him to, and she was not offended.

"Where shall we go? Shall I pick the place?" She fastened her seat belt and drew it tight across her lap before she turned the ignition key. As the car glided away from the curb, Julie was relieved that no one was in the street to see her with the apple. Old Mrs. Sewall next door was especially a gossip; she would have told her nephew.

She avoided the center of town, proceeding by way of several back streets to a narrow country road that led to Byers' Lake. Some houses she had to pass; some porches people rocked on, their figures silhouetted in yellow light from parlors. She was excited both by the apple's presence and by the risk of being watched and wondered about.

"I've been thinking about you all day," she told the apple. "Can you believe that?"

She glanced over at him. Something smug about his posture pleased her—as if he were proud to have been in her thoughts.

Now she was driving perhaps a little too fast. The apple shifted his position, and she let up on the accelerator.

"I'm sorry the roads are so bumpy out here," she told him. "Wouldn't you like to use your safety belt?"

Then she realized what she had said.

"Oh, dear; I didn't mean that. Really, I'm not a reckless driver." She smiled at him; he was unperturbed.

When she reached the western shore of Byers' Lake, Julie skirted the edge of the water until she came to a familiar place. She parked facing the lake. An orange moon was rising. On either side of the car were a number of wooden benches ranged along the waterside, and beyond them low wooden tables and empty oil drums for wastepaper. No picnickers at this hour. She had often come here with her father; here they had eaten butter cookies and fished for perch in the motionless lake. She had used the cookies for bait.

"I bring all my boyfriends here," Julie said. She released the buckle of the seat belt and turned to face the apple. "That's a kind of joke," she added.

The apple wasn't laughing. That was something you never knew, Julie thought; whether you could count on any of them to have a sense of humor—or exactly what kind of humor they did have a sense for. He seemed, certainly, aloof; yet she imagined in his reserve a gentleness.

"To be honest, I've never brought *any* boyfriends here. I don't have any—not to speak of."

She watched the apple closely, curious to see what effect this confession might have. None. She wanted to go on and explain, without conceit, that it was not because she was unattractive that she did not have lovers; she would not have used that word aloud. She wanted to make clear to the apple that choice had secured her freedom, that necessity had nothing to do with her. Looking straight at him, it was as if she were facing a slightly distorted mirror in which she could verify the evidence from her opinions. Her face in the light of the swollen moon gave itself back from him as if etched on wax. She would, truly, have spoken, only that her image began unexpectedly to cloud over.

"Oh, my heavens," she said, "you're cold. Forgive me; I'll put the top up."

She turned the ignition key and engaged the mechanism which set the top in motion. Odd. She felt an almost physical hitch in her thoughts, an apprehension again, but it was all right; she never had remembered to fasten down the canvas covering over the collapsed top, so now it rose up freely, whirring, leaning back and then thrusting forward like a long-necked bird. The top settled upon the windscreen and went silent.

"I forget about fall—how crisp it gets at night." She trusted this would excuse her lack of forethought. The apple sat motionless; beads of moisture lay grayly upon him.

Julie was obliged, then, to lean across the seat to latch the top into place. Doing so brought her into contact with the apple—nothing more than the touch of an instant, and yet something profoundly physical. Not that the apple responded. Worse, he yielded—a response more positive than mere toleration of her body's restrained weight. She didn't know what to make of *that*. The car top secured, she drew back, vowing not to mention her misgivings.

"There," she said, stupidly.

The windows were still open, yet the simple fact of a roof overhead made the car smaller and confined its atmosphere. The smell of the apple became insistent; before closing the car, she had not noticed it, but now she noticed nothing else. The air was heady and sweet—palpable, like cider. The glass of the windshield steamed with it, or it was her eyes watering. She could not put from her mind the sensation of having touched the apple. She forgot her promise to herself.

"I don't want you to think it was anything but an accident," she said. He would know what she was referring to; after all, he *had* yielded. "I'm not a very deliberate person." That was true. She was a person of no intentions. She tried to shut up and grit her teeth. She wished to God she had not met the apple tonight.

"It was a silly little bit of jostling," she said. *Here I go:* "If I'd really *intended* to touch you—"

And there were her hands, moving, one following the other. She saw herself put out her right hand toward the apple, first the fingertips and then the palm closing against the damp skin beside her. The left hand beside the right, pressing, bold. What was odd, now, was that she could feel him breathing—or something like breathing. Under her opened hands the apple throbbed, sang. A pulse like an engine. Curiously, dumbly, she was offended; instead of drawing back, she grew angry.

"I don't know what you're thinking," she said, and her teeth were still gritted, so that the words seemed to be shaped from a voice not her own.

The apple was silent. Julie found herself thinking: *Bump, bump, bump.* She laughed, feeling the laughter throbbing to her hands as if a counter to the machinery in the apple. She felt much stronger. She felt superior.

"Remember," she whispered, "that it's me who asked for this evening. Not you. You remember that." To prove her power over him, she turned her nails under and against the skin of the apple. She let the nail-edges break through. With all her strength she raked her hands downward until her wrists met the seat-cushion. Then she backed away, against her door. The odor of apple in the car turned heavy as syrup. *Oh my God*, she thought; *what have I done to him?* She sat drugged.

For a long time she waited, wordless, watching the apple. He was changed, as if he had suddenly grown old, as if he were tired or dying. Julie did not understand her own feelings; she could not imagine his. The orange moon went to white and floated slowly up out of sight above the field of view defined by the windshield. The lake turned to chalk. The benches and tables and oil drums assumed changed outlines in the fickle light. Hours passed.

At last, as if she were waking from a trance, she said: "I'm sorry. You'd better get out; I have to go home."

Because the apple did not move, Julie got out of the car and walked around to the other side. The bent grass was damp across her ankles.

"I am sorry," she said. She opened the door; the apple tottered at the edge of the seat, then dropped into the grass. She closed the door. The sound the apple had made when he struck the ground hung in the night like a single heartbeat. She looked down only long enough to make out the thin, puffy scars—who could have dreamed how vulnerable he was?—and then she got back into the car and drove wildly away.

By the time she reached home, the lights in her mother's bedroom had gone out and the house was dark. She parked the car at the curb, rolled up the windows, and chose to cross the lawn to smother the sounding of her heels. She slipped through the front door into the hall. The house creaked with silence; there was no point in waking her mother to tell what she had done. She climbed the stairs in her stocking feet—certain, anyway, that her mother would not understand.

Once safely in her room, Julie lay on top of the bed and had a cigarette. She was trembling; she was not ready to sleep. All night her hands hummed with the recollection of touching the apple. When she put her right hand near her face to inhale from the cigarette, the odor of apple throbbed from beneath her nails. She did not sleep; she could not even close her eyes. The sun rose redly; the October foliage on trees across the way took fire. She got up from the bed when she heard her mother moving downstairs.

In the kitchen, Julie found coffee and toast ready on the table. Her mother puttered near the sink, rattling cups and cutlery. Her mother said:

"Do you want some juice?"

"No, Mother."

"Isn't that the same outfit you had on last night?"

"Yes."

"Whatever time did you get home? Didn't you go to bed at all?"

"I don't know, Mother."

"Don't know *what?*"

Julie put sugar in the coffee and stirred. "What time I got home," she said.

"Nothing's wrong, it it?"

"No; nothing."

Her mother rattled dishes, closed cupboard doors, ran loud water from the taps. Julie sipped at the coffee.

"I wish you'd brought that boy in last night," her mother said. "You know I like to meet your friends."

"I'm sorry. We were late."

"I do worry about you, dear."

Julie nodded. She pushed the coffee cup aside; she lit a cigarette and looked at her watch. Seven-thirty. The apple had been lying in the grass for hours and hours. She brought the cigarette to her lips, and realized she hadn't washed her hands for breakfast.

"I'd really better be getting to work," Julie announced. She pushed her chair back from the table.

"You've got a good fifteen minutes yet."

"Well, I have an errand to do on the way."

"Have a second cup with Mother," her mother said.

Julie shook her head. She got up and went to the sink; she ran cold water over her hands and dried them on a dish towel.

"Will you be home for lunch?"

"I don't know. I'll call you."

She went upstairs for her purse, and stopped before the dresser mirror to put some order in her hair. As she came downstairs and left the house, she heard her mother shaking the kitchen.

Because she was alone, Julie drove straight through town on a shorter route to the lake. She rolled down her window to air out the car. It was a warm day—of an Indian summer sort—though from the water spots on the hood of the car she guessed there had been frost overnight. She smoked and listened to the radio. Instead of being early for work, she would be late. She felt compelled to see the apple again, as if she might make an opportunity for apology.

At the lake she was scrupulously careful to park a few yards further up the shore; Lord knew she didn't want to run him over, too. She switched off the ignition, stubbed the cigarette in the ashtray. Getting out, she noticed the same gray blemish on her white shoe; she paused to rub it with the heel of her palm. The dark spot endured.

Julie had no trouble finding the apple, though she was shocked to see him. He lay stem down in the yellow grass, and the scars she had inflicted faced up at her. They were horribly brown—as if the apple were made of painted metal, rusting outward from hidden flaws. The cold weather of the night before had altered him. His skin, which last night had held her in its dark mirror, was loosened and coarse. Wrinkles, like the contractions on water freezing, had appeared on him. Julie knelt over him.

"I wish I hadn't hurt you," she said. Nothing else. She couldn't tell if he heard her, or if he was listening. She did not touch him. Perhaps he wasn't alive.

She was late to work by nearly forty minutes. The other girls were at their typewriters, their backs straight, their heads tipped primly toward their copy-work. Julie sat at her own desk and slid her purse into a bottom drawer. She arranged papers. She drew together letter sheets and carbons, and fed them into the typewriter.

"*Dear Sir:*" she typed.

Mrs. Sewall's nephew came out of a door at the far end of the long aisle of typists. He squinted straight at her and came forward. Beside her, he said:

"Here you are. I was worried. I called your mother about you."

"I had something to do on the way," Julie said. She turned back the sheets of paper in the machine and typed the day's date. She could not think properly about the letter; she thought about the apple and what she had done to him.

"Your mother *said* you were doing an errand," Mrs. Sewall's nephew went on.

"Yes, I was." She did not dislike him, but he made her nervous by his attention. He brought her a habit of small presents, like a schoolboy flattering his teacher.

"I'm glad you weren't ill," he said.

He went back to the office he had come out of. Julie opened the bottom drawer and rummaged through her purse for cigarettes and matches. She carried them with her to the ladies' room, where she lounged against a windowsill and smoked and watched another girl comb her hair. The light through the window leaned against the back of her neck.

The day went by slowly; she skipped lunch to make up for her lateness. Several times she visited the ladies' room and on each occasion felt the touch of the light slightly changed. She failed to finish her letter. When five o'clock came, she did not drive directly home, but went to Byers' Lake. She parked a short distance from the apple and sat until dusk, watching him from the car.

Her mother remarked on the hour.

"I stayed over to make up some time," Julie told her. "I was tardy this morning."

"Where did you go?"

"It doesn't matter, Mother." She ate some of the cold supper, then went to her room to remember the apple. She sat by the dresser lamp and trimmed her nails. She lay awake in bed and tried not to smoke.

"Your father wouldn't have let you moon around like this," her mother told her the next morning.

"I know."

"I think you're carrying on with this boy."

"I can't help *that*," Julie said.

On the third morning her mother said: "Mrs. Sewall's nephew calls me every time you're late to work. I want you to know; we're beginning to wonder."

Julie shrugged.

When she drove to the lake on Friday evening, the world was much changed. The seasons were in motion. During the week the temperature had fallen slowly, the nights were chilling, the trees all over town had dropped their dry, brown leaves into the gutters. Though she tried to resist wearing a coat, Julie found that the weathers of Byers' Lake were beginning to leave her miserable with cold; today she had dressed warmly. Rather that, than to give up the ritual of her visits to the apple, a few minutes spent with him each morning and evening. Sometimes she sat in the dead grass beside him; sometimes she sat in the car nearby, and grew accustomed to the stifled smells of the car's heater. She talked to the apple—about how the silences between herself and her mother became more natural; about how the lack of sleep no longer left her exhausted through the daylight hours. She talked to the apple about guilt; she believed he was alive, and listening. She believed he understood.

She parked close by and got out of the car. A wind was up from the northeast, roughening the lake, pushing out wraiths of gray cloud from the opposite shore. The color was out of the woods; islands of spruce and pine stood more black than green. She turned up her collar and went to the apple.

He was hideous. Every day grown less like what she had met on the first night, now he was scarcely recognizable. His redness was drained off into hollow muddles of brown, the heady odor of his flesh gone sour on the wind. His skin was like a shell, his body translucent as gelatin in a filmy envelope. His roundness sagged into the earth. She had long since ceased to be offended by the changes in him, but now, for the first time, the sight of him moved her to despair. *Dear God*, thought Julie; *oh, dear God*. Her eyes into the wind stung with tears. She reached out to him.

"I'm sorry, I swear. If only I could have you back—"

She blubbered the words. Her hands closed over the apple, lifted him, felt him giving way between her palms. The soft, cold marrow melted against her and oozed through her fingers. She screamed; she could not let go. She fell forward to her knees and pressed the apple close against the front of her coat, her body rocking and shaking from her sobs. Something touched her arm—a pressure not a ghost, a real touch. She looked up. Mrs. Sewall's nephew stood above her; his hand squeezed her elbow. The man's face swam in the shallows of her sight, and she could not understand what he said ·over the sounds she was making. She lost her balance and fell; she thought her mother was standing by the car, watching, horrified. Mrs. Sewall's nephew reached down. Julie rested her cheek on the ground and embraced the apple.

"It isn't true," she whimpered. She felt the apple against her heart, *bump, bump, bump*; the warmed pulp dribbled over the backs of her hands. "It isn't what you think."

The *United States*

Later we will tell how we happen to be here in the first-class lounge of the *United States*, but for the time being: there are three of us, and we are, incredibly, the only persons seated in a space that is at least fifteen meters wide and perhaps twenty-five meters long. At this moment a steward is coming to our table with a tray of martinis, two up and one on the rocks. Even after last night, Patricia and I are too effete to sip our drinks around ice; Donald believes that a drink on the rocks lasts longer and is less debilitating than a drink served without ice in a stemmed glass—he truly thinks about such things— while I am presently far more concerned for the textures and warmths slightly above Patricia's shapely knee; this sort of thing is a constant preoccupation with me, ever since Patricia's husband sailed for America on board the *Olympia*, three months ago. And now the steward is beside our table, arranging the drinks before us; each martini costs one dollar US. All of us are offended by the price.

I wonder if we remembered to tell you that the year is 1953.

We have driven to the ship in Patricia's husband's Jaguar Mark VII Saloon—a quite remarkable machine, perhaps a trifle short on headroom, but lovely nevertheless. The motorcar is a deep burgundy in color; it has wire wheels and those wide whitewalls hardly anyone will know in twenty years, until all at once they begin to "come back," and its interior appointments (as they say) especially include tan leather upholstery whose odor is in its way as heady as the scent

Patricia is wearing, and whose appearance is as rich but understated as the white linen suit she has chosen to wear today. It's a hell of a car, really. The speedometer changes colors in ascending kilometer ranges, turning from green to soft orange to a suffusion of anxious red. Donald and I have been driving the Jaguar for the past two months—Patricia is afraid of motorcars and cannot drive—and just last week we reached 180 kilometers per hour on the *autobahn* from Bremen to Hamburg. God, what a car it is. Then, as now, Patricia huddled against me in the back seat and helped me place my hands so the outrageous speeds would make neither of us nervous.

Did we say the ship is docked in Bremerhaven? During the summer months—the "season"—the *United States* docks here every two or three weeks. If I am not mistaken, she stops at Le Havre inbound and Southampton outbound—or it may be the other way around. In any event, her sister ship, the *America*, docks here all year. Whichever ship you choose, the tourist-class passage to New York costs 186 dollars US.

In 1953 a great many things seem possible. We are all young: Patricia is 24, Donald is 23, I am 23; our best estimate at this moment of a humid afternoon in July is that the English-speaking world is just our age, and that it is careless, unencumbered, bright, in superb good health, ready to try anything at least twice, and well enough off to afford anything genuinely worth the purchasing. Nothing will change our minds. Once, in a pellucid instant, Patricia has suggested to me that we shall for the rest of our lives retain this judgment of the world, and that whatever happens we will hug to ourselves our faith in our own *rightness*, our own *worthiness*. This extraordinary wisdom while she was teasing me and giggling at the shock on Donald's face.

In fact, our world-view is somewhat blurred as we leave from Patricia's apartment and set out to the Columbus Quai. There has been a farewell party; it began the afternoon of the day before, and it was a proper affair—with a guest list, formal invitations written out in Patricia's artful little hand, a time span (3:30 to 5:30) specified, and a gorgeous subtle punch concocted mostly from champagne and vodka. Some twenty or so guests: A/2C and Mrs. Bradley Archer, whose mutual ambition is to enter the diplomatic service; A/2C James Neubauer and the Fräulein Ingeborg Theisse; S/Sgt Stanley ("Stosh") Borzyskowski; A/1C Mark Greenawald, who has dedicated his life to finding and marrying the richest girl in the Cincinnati-Covington area; A/B Gerald Barker, a gambler (poker, especially seven-card stud); three Special Services hostesses—Jean, Virginia, and Constance Elaine—; Carlotte and Heinz Schmitt, the German nationals who own the building, who are Patricia's landlady and landlord, whose punch recipe it is that we have followed and praised; and (finally) a German girl no one seems ever to have met before whose full name is Gertrud Maria Magdalena Schüssler, and whose unclothed body will some time be described—by Greenawald—as "purest gold."

And for all our mutual worthiness, the American air force is the sole deep occasion for our meeting here on Burgomeister-Schmidt-Strasse 29, Bremerhaven, Bremen Enclave, West Germany, on Saturday the 11th of July, in the Year of our Lord Nineteen Hundred and Fifty-Three.

Pros't, Schatz.

This scene: It is the day before the sailing of the *United States*, about halfway through the farewell party at Patricia's apartment. The heat in the apartment is beyond endurance; on the hall staircase leading upward to the Schmitt rooms we are strewn like toys, sweating, nursing our drinks. No one left at 5:30; at seven, Neubauer and Fräulein Theisse flagged a Mercedes taxi and directed its driver to the Butterfly Bar, where they bought a quantity of hot *bockwurst*, then returned to the Burgomeister-Schmidt-Strasse address at about 8:15. Neubauer claims to have made love to Fräulein Theisse three times during the errand—once going and twice returning—and he has marched the taxi driver upstairs as witness. Neubauer is a short man, Fraulein Theisse is a plump lady; anything is possible. We are all grateful for the *wurst*.

This scene: We are sprawled on the staircase, sweating and belching.

Someone at the top of the stairs has actually fallen asleep. We hear him snoring; we hear the punch glass topple out of his grasp and roll down two steps before Mrs. Archer, Caroline, pushes it through the balustrade uprights with her elbow. The glass bounces before it breaks in front of Patricia's open door. An odd sight; it is as if the glass has levitated from the hall floor and burst in midair. At the sound of the breaking, Constance Elaine rushes out to ask what the noise is. She is barefooted, and when we finally get her to the military hospital a bemused German doctor has to take seven stitches in her foot.

Finally, this scene: The staircase is like the vanes in some sort of vertical heat duct, and we are half-lying, half-fainting against varnished surfaces. Patricia is on the fifth step, sprawled, leaning against the wall, her eyes half-closed and gazing—apparently—at the light fixture above us. She is humming; in her left hand is a nearly empty champagne glass, the bowl cradled in her fingers, the stem free and swaying like a pendulum. It is Patricia who once explained that you can tell whether a woman is married or unmarried by the way she holds a stemmed glass. If she has anything to explain to me now, or if she is even *thinking* of anything, no evidence presents itself. I can see in her half-hidden eyes the reduced reflections of the light bulb overhead, can make out the tune she is humming—"You Belong to Me," an out-of-date Jo Stafford song—can assume from the looseness of her wrist that she is only floating down the long staircase into her concealed world of memory and idle daydream. I am seated below her, on the second step. I have laid my head back between her thighs, my left temple resting against the bare flesh above her stocking-top and below the white (silk?) panties she wears, the back of my head pillowed on her belly. In my left hand I hold what remains of a water glass of punch; my right arm is laid along Patricia's right leg, my hand stroking her ankle. I cannot begin to describe how drenched with sweat I am, how lethargic I feel. If the world ended now, if the sky fell, if the Russians attacked . . . it would all be one and indifferent. The heat between Patricia's legs is like the sun's, the softness of her thighs is clouds and flowers; against the back of my head is the throbbing of a secret engine waiting to drive the world wherever it desires. I imagine her sheer sexual energy directed toward no end, an idling, a dim green light in our shared darkness. I say to Patricia:

"The punch is drunk up."

She stirs; I ride, giddy, with her small movement. "Oh, I know," Patricia says. "This bunch of people. . . ." She shifts the champagne glass to her right hand, strokes the stem between the thumb and fingers of her left. I am looking up at her, my head far back; I see her face through the curve of her glass, and I feel the hem of her skirt over my right ear. The hot odor between Patricia's thighs is the ozone of that obscure engine driving us, driving me.

But we are all under inhuman pressures. In the spring a British Lancaster was shot down by MIG-17's of the Soviet Air Army (Rostock) in the corridor between Hamburg and Berlin. Soon after, two American jet fighters were intercepted and destroyed along the Czech border by MIG's of the Air Army (Zwickau). We monitored both incidents, in each case listening to the Soviet ground controller vector his fighters to the target, hearing the command to open fire, startled to realize—because the appropriate code words are so rare —*the attack is real, people are dying.* We sit in our barracks rooms all through the wet spring months, drinking Tuborg beer and talking of war—of pre-emptive nuclear strikes, of our closeness to the enemy zone (ten air minutes), of our own importance, of whether we are interested in dying. From Rotenburg, in the British Zone, where our officers go to record the flying time necessary to keep their flight pay, it is said that both the British and American pilots in their ray-shaped Hawkers fly hedgehopping missions across the zonal border to provoke the Soviet radar; we find this an exciting notion, fun. We are all Romance, espionage, cloak and dagger, ready to have the life coaxed out of us. If the tanks roll in East Berlin, may we not someday march with the citizens against them?

What is immediate, of course, is that we finish the farewell party for Patricia. She is returning to the States, to her husband, and Donald and I must drive her in her husband's Jaguar to the Columbus Quai.

Our lives have a particular purpose.

I say this ("Our lives have purpose.") to Patricia in the living room of her apartment. It is exceedingly late—actually Sunday morning, the day of her departure, around three o'clock. We are lying on the floor together; I cannot tell where the others are, though in some dim corner of my brain I must know they are still in the building, in the hallway, probably even in the room with us. The truth is that we have all drunk so much—first the punch, and then a putting-together of all the wines, whiskies, aromatics, liqueurs, and mixes left in the apartment, all poured mindlessly into the emptied punch bowl and then parceled out among the party—we have all drunk so much, we are deep inside ourselves and scarcely able to connect with a world discrete from us. When I say, "Our lives have purpose," Patricia says, "Mmm," and turns her face toward me; I touch my lips to her forehead and taste sweat, delicately salt.

Somewhere in time she has changed her clothes. As I touch her it seems to me she is wearing only a robe, a black robe with red and orange appliqué flowers patterned on the lapels, a robe tied at her waist by a black slender belt frayed at the ends. I put one hand against the robe—is it silk?—and feel her breasts beneath the smooth fabric; they are unexpectedly soft, as if she were older, as if she were someone's mother. She raises her left hand and rests it on the back of my fingers—not to take my hand away, but neither to encourage me. I kiss her eyes, the closed lids; I kiss her cheeks, the corners of her mouth. Now I kiss her full on the mouth, open her lips, insist my tongue between her teeth.

She bites my tongue.

When I pull my head back, startled, she opens her eyes to read my face. What she sees makes her laugh, and no matter what I do or say I cannot stop her laughing.

Patricia's husband is one of those who had no dealings with the city's whores, who visited the bars rarely, who lived even under the obligations of a military occupation (and a military presence looking ahead) as if the barracks were a row of brownstones and the parqueted floors of our modest rooms were aglow under the reading lamps of The Club. Before Patricia flew to Germany to marry him, he was my roommate and tried to teach me grace, to encourage me to recognize style. Every afternoon at four—unless we worked the day shift out at Squadron Operations—he mixed a pitcher of martinis; we sat, like two gentlemen of Cambridge, sipping our drinks, listening to Barbara Carroll or Mabel Mercer or Hugh Shannon or the most-prized Greta Keller, not so much weighing the problems of our world as settling them.

Once in a great while Donald joined us for cocktails, and it was Donald who, only a week before Patricia's arrival at the Bremen airfield, innocently brought her bridegroom into the Butterfly for his famous encounter with Ingeborg Theisse—plump, ripe Ingeborg, with the reddest hair, the best English, of all the prostitutes in the Enclave.

"They say he's cherry," we told her.

"Now wait a second," said the groom.

"I can give you advice," Ingeborg said. "Always ride high; the woman has more sensation high."

"I'll remember."

"But honestly, you never touched a woman?" Ingeborg took his hand and drew it under her skirt—a black skirt, long, but slit at the sides. He tried to pull away, but she is a woman of great strength and held him; she pressed his hand up between her legs—he blushing, she smiling—and rocked against him. All of us looked part wise, part perplexed.

Then: "God, please! Please leave me alone!"

He startled us, there was such pain in the words, and when we looked at his face we saw tears bright in his eyes and wet on his cheeks. Ingeborg stopped moving, stopped smiling. She backed away from him and slid his hand out from under her clothes; he held the hand up as if it were hurt. No one said much, and poor Donald looked like death.

Later it was Donald who took Ingeborg to her room—no ships were in port—and the rest of us, Stanley and Gerald and Mark, went back to the barracks. In the room—it was after midnight; we were having a last beer while the phonograph played "One Touch of

Venus"—Patricia's husband said to me:

"Don't ever tell Patsy."

So. Just a few weeks ago his father died and he took an early discharge to go home to Kansas City to manage a packing house.

Years from now, when we hold reunions or meet accidentally at an air terminal or bump into one another at conventions, we will sit in a dark corner of some barroom nothing like the Butterfly and talk about Bremerhaven—though it is impossible, in 1953, to know what our recollections will come to. Will we remember our first days in the city: October, rain blowing in off the North Sea (a Sea that is invisible to us beyond the great mounded-earth dikes), a cold whose dampness seeps to the very marrow? The rubble, seven and eight years after the end of the war, pulled to the sides of streets only beginning to be repaved, and the first new, raw apartment houses rising beside basements reeking of brown water? Or the stories we hear from everyone, American and German, about the retaliation bombing of the city after Coventry—how the British Havilands strafed and bombed from less than a hundred meters of altitude, leveling the Hafenstrasse, wasting most of the residential city, leaving wholly untouched the port facilities and the Marine barracks where all of us came to live? The foresight of the Allies: it makes us proud. Surely we will remember the whores—Inges and Margots and Karlas and Erikas—who drink and laugh with us, who know our secret projects better than our officers, who charge for their favors 300 marks when the merchant ships are in, 20 when they are not?

This scene, the last with Patricia ashore: It is shortly after dawn, a windless morning, gray from a fog that will not burn away until nearly noon. The apartment is emptied of revelers—except for Donald, asleep on a sofa under the bay window. Everything is a shambles. Glasses are on all the furniture surfaces—chair arms, table tops, bookshelves, hassocks—and on floors and carpets. A lot of things, liquid and not, have been spilled; if you look out the doorway into the hall you see glassware, paper plates, crumpled napkins, as if someone had overturned a trash barrel at the head of the stairs; the air is heavy with stale cigarette smoke, the odors of old perfume and fancy drink.

Patricia is awake first, and rouses me out of a heavy-headed sleep; my body has settled into some shape that has no life of its own—a piece of sod, a stone, a rug rolled for storage. I groan and, groaning and hearing myself, open my eyes to see where the sound comes from. Patricia and I are still joined, our bare legs stuck together with sweat, the two of us even holding hands like children on a hayride. Her robe is open and twisted under us; I am in my blue shirt, my black socks, but the rest of my uniform is in a heap in the seat of a soft chair near the kitchen door. My tongue hurts me. I remember being bitten. I remember Patricia laughing. I remember nothing else.

"What time is it?" I try to find my watch, but it is on my left wrist, and my left wrist is under Patricia's back. I try to move her, and as she rolls away from me it is like adhesive tape being ripped off my skin. Our bellies and thighs are red, our hair drenched. She reaches out to me, leans over and kisses me.

"What a hellish country this is," she says hoarsely.

We help each other to stand. We bathe and dress. We wake Donald.

We forgive ourselves everything, though we have endless parties, drink too much, make frequent fools of ourselves in the eyes of the German nationals. Sometimes we have fistfights with the infantry—our barracks neighbors, our comrades in arms. Other times we quarrel with the naval detachment nearby. Mostly we tyrannize the civilians; we say things like "Who won this war?" (though we were far too young to have fought it) and we sell cigarettes and coffee and sometimes currency on the black markets. Also we travel. We go to Amsterdam and smoke marijuana for the first time in our lives. We go to Copenhagen, spend a lot of time and money in the after-hours clubs, and stay at the Roxy Hotel because the girls are lovely and speak English. Are we not the perfect ambassadors of freedom?

The worst times are political—the rumors that our squadron will be the first evacuated in the event of war, that if there is no time for evacuation our officers have orders to shoot us. It is a glamorous notion. We argue by the hour: Would you let yourself be shot? Would you surrender? If you were tortured would you reveal military secrets? Then our lives seem rich but desperate. It is said that Lieutenant Wieczorek, the watch officer when an orange alert was called during the defection of a Polish fighter pilot, suffered a nervous breakdown and tried to kill himself.

The best times are parties on shipboard—but not American ships, whose liquor prices are too high. The ships of German, Greek, Swedish, Canadian registry—these are fine. Some ships become traditions: the North German Lloyd's liner *Berlin*, the old *Gripsholm*, is a regular—about 12 cents for the finest Scotch whiskey, always crowded, plenty of "nice" local girls. For all departure parties you only need to arrange a visitor's pass with a member of the ship's crew. That is simple, and it is the least the crewman can do after inflating the economy hereabouts.

The three of us sit in the barren first-class lounge of the *United States*, drinking our expensive martinis and finding it difficult to make conversation. I am amazed at how lovely and rested Patricia looks after last night, and I have said so; Donald agreed with me. Donald has promised we will be most careful with the Jaguar until we bring it to be shipped aboard the *America* next week, and I have seconded the promise; I have reminded her that we shipped home her husband's MG-TD without mishap two months ago. Patricia has confided that in an odd way, much as she loves her husband and much as she is looking forward to Kansas City and the nice new home now being built for her, she will miss dirty old Bremerhaven and all the good friends—she squeezes my hand—left behind. She says that at the very least she will try to make the people back home understand that even if we are not dying in Korea, we are all doing an important job—we are in Europe for a *purpose*. I look at Donald; he is making a face, a horrible face. "You are all preventing a *big* war," Patricia says.

An hour later we are standing on the cobbled quai, waving up at Patricia as the *United States* slowly pivots away from shore, the

German tugs nudging her into the brown waters that flow from the North Sea. It has gotten very warm, and Patricia has taken off the long-sleeved jacket of her suit; the ruffles of her white blouse—is it silk, in this weather?—flutter as she waves down to us. There is so much noise, so many voices, music so loud to our left, that to shout more goodbyes would be useless. We only watch, and as the image of Patricia slowly diminishes in my sight I remember just for an instant what she was saying over martinis. Did she mean it? Could anyone?

A week later Donald and I drive the Mark VII Saloon back to Columbus Quai; it is going aboard the *America* for New York, where Patricia's husband will meet it and drive it to Kansas City. What a shame—I say this to Donald just after we have handed the car over to the dispatcher—what a terrible shame Patricia's husband will never be able to drive the car on U.S. roads at the speeds permitted on the new Bremen-Hamburg *autobahn*. Yes, says Donald, this motorcar is too good for him—too fast, too temperamental for the ZI. Sometimes Donald himself is too military, as when he adopts such jargon as *ZI*—for "Zone of the Interior"—when he means home, the States. Greenawald concurs. "A Chevy would satisfy that phoney," he says. Greenawald has hung around with us since the *United States* sailed, boring us endlessly with the precious golden skin of Gertrud Maria Magdalena Schüssler. We walk away from the car, preoccupied by speed and beauty, and drift up a flight of steps to the restaurant overlooking dockside.

The restaurant is crowded, but we find a table near a window. We order a Beck's and two Carlsbergs. "Really," Greenawald is saying, "when she took off her clothes I felt like King Midas; she was purest gold." Donald glances at me; I shrug. For myself, Patricia has been in and out of my head since the tugs pushed her ship into the channel of the Weser. Her languor, her textures, perhaps her wealth. . . .

We sit, drinking the beer, talking hardly at all. Once Donald points out the window, and I turn to see the Jaguar, cradled in raw wood, suspended from the cable of a crane slowly swiveling toward the *America*. I feel an odd, momentary churning in my stomach, and I hope they know to be careful. The auto looks like a plum, rounded and vulnerable, dangling from an artificial branch. In ten minutes it is out of our sight.

On the way to the center of the city I am absorbed in 1953 and our curious lives away from the familiar—what serious things concern us, what friends we have met, what confident future we look ahead to. I believe I have become, like Donald, too solemn for my own good, and when the yellow streetcar passes the Butterfly I motion the others to get off and follow me into the bar. I want to look for Ingeborg: I think I want to make fun of Greenawald's golden girlfriend with all her pretentious saintly names.

Norma Jean Becoming Her Admirers

She is knocking on doors. I hear her, in the long hallway of the hotel, drawing nearer. Rap; rap, rap; rap, rap, RAP! A startling strength in her small wrists. It is my door at last, and I am quick to open it.

Hi, she says. She is unconscionably fresh; her blonde hair is wanton, tousled, awry; her smile stops my heart; her skin is so pale I believe I am confronting a wraith. Help me, she says. She walks toward me, through me, into the room behind me. Help me.

I turn. The sun is blossoming through the windows with such force that I am blinded and she is invisible. A moment later it is midnight, the overhead light is on, there is nothing left of her but the white petals of her clothing in a heap on the carpet.

When I go into the bedroom I am astonished to see her lying on the bed—my bed, the bed I have not allowed the maid to make up since I checked in three days ago. She is naked. I avert my eyes. I hear her say:

Do you have veins?

I tell her everyone has veins.

She explains that she means veins on the backs of hands, that it is the obvious presence of such veins—blue, sometimes—which makes a person look old, that one can often calculate the age of a woman, possibly also of a man, by examining the veins on the backs of the hands.

I tell her this is to some degree a revelation to me, and that liver spots are also useful clues to age in both men and women.

She indicates that liver spots are of no moment, but that she has a method for getting rid of veins.

Excision, I suggest.

She pretends confusion.

I elaborate, proposing that a strong woman might work a thin skewer under the veins on the back of the hand, and then twist the skewer so the veins would pull free like the roots of a young willow.

She is horrified, and says so. No, she says, no. I don't mean *really* to get rid of the veins; I mean to *seem* to really get rid of the veins.

I nod. It is a perfectly lucid distinction.

All you have to do is hold your hands high in the air and shake them. Shake until your hands feel numb, until the skin seems to be humming to itself. The veins will disappear, like magic. The backs of your hands will be perfectly smooth, perfectly clear, white as a young girl's hands.

Incredible, I say.

You have to look, she insists. *Look* at them.

I look. The hands are delicate and pale and unmarked; the arms are creamy, the fine hairs light brown in the shadows; the shoulders are like melting glaciers, the breasts tremble in the nets of their own veins, the belly is a mound of biblical wheat, the thighs birches, the feet small wings. . . . I look at the hands; now the blue veins are swelling up under the skin, the hands are aging. I feel tears in my eyes. When I tell her I do not want her to grow older, I do not want her to die, she blushes and turns her face to the pillow.

I discover she is hungry for knowledge, but she is not bookish— this revealed as we sit on the balcony after supper. Our talk turns to the great authors, or—as she would have it—the great teachers. She sits across the table from me in a traveling-gray negligee, a forelock of bright hair tumbling onto her forehead, her unrouged lips pursed over the cards in her lap.

I'll give you an Emile Zola for an Unamuno, I tell her.

No, she says; I have a Zola. Do you have a Turgenev?

I look. Yes, I have a Turgenev.

Sitting or standing?

Standing.

Oh, good! She destroys me with a smile that animates all her features, and we exchange the cards. She pretends to kiss it.

Have you a duplicate Dostoevsky? I ask.

Oh yes, she says. What will you swap me for it?

How about an Ezra Pound?

She giggles.

Two Ezra Pounds, I say.

She puts on a face to chide me. Really now, she says.

It's true, of course. The Ezra Pounds are a drug on the market; I remember as a child my disappointment when I unwrapped the gum and there was Pound again. It was almost always Pound or Hemingway or Sandburg; when you were flipping cards nearest the wall after school, and you were in a losing streak, it was those cards you gambled first and didn't mind giving up. Or scarcely minded.

You're a shrewd swapper, I tell her.

She grins and hugs herself.

Now that she has been in my room for several days, I believe it is appropriate to tell her how much I would like to make love to her.

She turns away.

Think of it, I say, as a kind of worship, a litany of touching, a way of entering the universe.

She folds her hands in her lap.

I'm only human, I tell her.

She hunches forward and presses her lips against her clasped fingers.

We've shared so much, I remind her. Why should we omit anything that might please us?

She lies against the heaped-up pillows, draws her legs close, shuts her eyes.

Come on, I coax. Let me love you within an inch of your life. I rest my hand on her silken thigh. I feel her tremble.

I'm a great round ball, she says, riding on a sea that goes on forever. If I relax, if I just let go, I'll roll off this bed and float to the end

of time. She opens her eyes and looks at me archly.
No, she says. Certainly not.

I teach her:
Euclid alone has looked on Beauty bare.
I teach her:
              Her feet
Practise a tinker shuffle
Picked up on a street.
I teach her:
I knew a woman, lovely in her bones.
I teach her:
Full of her long white arms and milky skin
He had a thousand times remembered sin.
I teach her:
One's grand flights, one's Sunday baths,
One's tootings at the weddings of the soul
Occur as they occur.
And I teach her:
You shall above all things be glad and young.
She teaches me:
I am nor drink nor food,
Nor any man's good.
I ask the author. She shrugs and makes a mincing mouth.

On the next-to-last day she lets me watch her shower. It is like
theatre—the bathroom as proscenium stage, the glass of the shower
stall a curtain not parted until play's end. Thus I am no more witness to the action than if I had stayed entirely away. By the time she
begins, the hot water has already steamed the tempered glass; by the
time she concludes, the room is so misted I have no more than a
moment's glimpse of her towel. In between—the performance itself
—I enjoy light and shadow, gold and green images dancing; I
breathe the moistened clean air; I am tipsy from the fragrances of
lotion and soap. I think: I am the ghost of Herod.
Afterward, dressed, she lets me go with her to the drugstore.

Heads turn and mouths open as we promenade. Men whistle and groan out the rolled-down windows of their taxis. Women look darts and daggers. Small children, too young to know anything, point and seem wise. I am still so dizzied by her company, by the weight of her hand on my sleeve, that I totter as I walk. She grips my arm and steadies me as I stumble over a curb.

Don't they threaten you? I say to her.

Who?

The men. Don't the men threaten you?

She smiles. They flatter me, distract me; sometimes they humiliate me with their daydreams.

How do you know the daydreams? I ask.

How does a seed know the clouds? she answers.

So in thirteen days and nights we have left this hotel suite only the once. We have called to the kitchen for our food, rung the front desk for newspapers, fixed our attention on late television as if it were a desirable guest in our lives. We are amazed at our self-sufficiency, our patience with each other; it happens that we are able to share our surroundings without quarrel—that on the odd-numbered nights she has the bed, on the even-numbered the sofa; that in the morning she is first in the bathroom, while at night I am the first; that she does not read the entertainment pages, and I read nothing else.

We never touch each other. In between the meals and the papers, the sleep and the television films, we talk—usually about serious matters. When I catch her with her hands flopping in the air above her head, I mock her by putting my fingertips at my temples and drawing tight the skin of my face. I tell her I look exactly as I did when I was a high school boy; and I do. When I release the skin, I am my old self, hollow-eyed and soft-mouthed and crow-footed. She in her turn is pensive; she smokes cigarettes and talks in a private voice about mortality, about the age at which bruises heal slowly and never entirely vanish. Once, even, she reads to me from the back of the Dostoevsky card:

Forty years is a lifetime; forty is profound old age. It's

indecent, it's vulgar and immoral, to live past forty; nobody
does it except damned fools and failures.

She is sitting up in bed, naked and round-shouldered, and when she
asks me to fetch a glass of water for her pills, I slide the bathroom
tumbler out of its waxed-paper envelope without for an instant
imagining I can refuse her anything.

The Demonstration

From the time he started across the April-damp lawn to face a rebel for the first time in his life, Thomas Blessing was filled with the sense of what was at stake. In back of him the Eternal Hope Funeral Home cast its cool shade over his mission, the two-and-a-half-story structure seeming less like a place of commercial enterprise than an institution—an absolute symbol of the destiny of Man, of the peace and dignity and resignation which was the common lot of the great and the small. Eternal Hope was larger than time, larger than Blessing, certainly larger than a single addle-headed demonstrator afraid to meet his Maker. In a way the presence of one unexpected dissident with his placard threw into bold relief the immensity and solemnity of the Eternal Hope operation. Yet in another, more important, way a foolish old man was mocking the very existence of Eternal Hope. It was the latter insult Blessing intended to punish.

He stood before his adversary, and for the first time had a close look at him. Even seated in a folding chair, the man appeared to be tall, and something about the carriage of his gray head implied that the roundness of his shoulders was not to be counted for much. Possibly he cut a figure of considerable strength and self-possession— was a man easy to respect. *The more fool,* Blessing thought.

He introduced himself. "I am Thomas Blessing; I am the director of this funeral home, and you are interfering with my work."

The seated man inclined his head in a graceful—and most gracious—acknowledgment. "I am Laurence Garvey, emeritus professor of philosophy at the College."

You pompous scarecrow. Blessing coughed and put on his most ceremonious manner. "Professor Garvey, you are trespassing, and I am obliged to ask that you leave at once."

"But I explained to the other gentleman"—that would be Saunders, who had not been able to shoo him off—"the reasons for my fast," Garvey said; his voice was thin, like an old cricket's, but firm; he faced straight ahead and held his sign grimly. *No*, it said. Blessing made note that the lettering was Gothic. He felt thwarted.

"Now look here, Garvey," he said, "you can't picket Death. It comes. It always comes. No one knows that better than I do."

Garvey set his mouth. "Then I've nothing to lose," he said.

"And if you're just going to squat on my lawn and stop eating—" Blessing paused. "Is that really your plan?"

"It is."

"Then you'll drop dead all the sooner. You're defeating your own purpose."

"My friends at the nursing home will take care of me," Garvey said gently.

Obviously, thought Blessing, nothing was to be gained by trying to talk sensibly, standing in the young wet grass and ruining his shoes. He shook a finger in front of Garvey's impassive face. "You mark my words, Garvey," he said. "If you don't get off this property, I'll damn well show you what you've got to lose," and walked away feeling both rage and self-righteousness.

"I don't know what's happening to people," he said to Saunders. "A respectable old man like that, with not an ounce of consideration for anyone else. He must be seventy-five if he's a day; he ought to know better."

"He's a little strange," Saunders said.

"He's a little senile; that's what." Blessing smirked. "People will think we've run out of space inside."

Saunders smiled faintly.

"Well," said Blessing, sobering, "there's still work to be done. You'd better take Darrell and go fetch Mr. Foster before we waste the whole day." Foster was a farmer who lived at the other end of the county and had passed to his reward the night before. "I'll call to make the floral arrangements. And I'll call the police, too, if it comes to that."

When he had finished talking with the florist, Blessing returned to the window to see if Garvey had given up and gone home. He had not. Now, in fact, a number of other old people, both men and women, had appeared. All of them were milling around on the side lawn, attending to Garvey. Blessing watched carefully; they were feeding the old fool—soda crackers, it looked like, and a glass of water. *That's cheating*, he thought; *some fast.*

He slid the window open—a task that required considerable effort, for the window had not been opened since the summer before—and leaned out.

"You people get off that lawn," he shouted. "You can't loiter here. Go on back to the Seniory or I'll have you arrested."

He wasn't able to hear their answers, but what they said seemed uncomplimentary. Blessing forced the window shut and waited to see if Garvey and his cohorts would leave. After a few moments he was gratified to see the whole crowd—he had by now counted eleven of them besides the professor—move from the lawn to the sidewalk, but the gratification was short-lived. The group began walking, single file, back and forth in front of Eternal Hope. Only one person, a small, stooped man with a red bandana around his neck, went off in the direction of the Seniory.

Blessing's palms were damp with sweat. *They're actually picketing me!* A second placard had appeared, as if out of nowhere. *The Wages of Death Is Sin*, it stated.

He went directly to the telephone and called the mayor, who listened without comment to Blessing's story of the events outside Eternal Hope. "It's too damned much," Blessing said with some heat. "These idiots are getting out of bounds; I don't know what they'll do next." He requested police protection.

The mayor was reluctant. "I don't like trouble," he told Blessing, "even as a gift, and I'm certainly not going to ask for it. I can't have people thrown in jail for peaceful assembly."

"Peaceful!" Blessing exclaimed. "They're blocking my sidewalk."

The mayor persisted in his refusal to dispatch police. "Wait a while," he said. "If they do any damage to the place, then I'll shoot the riot squad over." And he hung up.

Blessing paced the room angrily, cursing the mayor under his breath. Finally he went into the Sincerity Chapel, where he sat with clenched fists and glared at the tiny altar with its candles glowing red inside glass chimneys. He could not think where to turn for help.

Meanwhile the pickets paraded—orderly, careful to respect the rights of the passers-by and the curious who shared the sidewalk with them. They remained an odd lot, and from time to time Blessing went to the front door to peep out and confirm their oddness. The red bandana had apparently gone for reinforcements, for now he counted seventeen picketers—twelve men and five women—and every one of them was ancient. Decrepit. The lame, the halt, and Blessing wouldn't have been surprised if a few of the seventeen were blind, clinging to the sign-carrier ahead of them. Couldn't even read the cards they held in their shaky hands. Blessing himself could scarcely read them. *No*, he could see, black and ornate in the hands of Professor Garvey. *We're People, Not Prospects*, in the unsteady grasp of a white-haired woman with a clubfoot. And to make matters worse, a mobile unit from the local television station had happened on the scene; Blessing saw it cruise past the crowd and draw to a stop half a block away.

His stomach felt queasy. He was a peaceable, comfortable man in a peaceable, comfortable business, and the sight of these otherwise sensible people taking their absurd stand against Nature seemed to affect his digestion. At the same time he was terribly sensitive to the practical problem of how such a furor must look to potential clients of the Eternal Hope. So much depended on the frame of mind of the client; it was so important that, by the time he or Saunders had left the client alone in the Selection Room, the client be convinced of Eternal Hope's ability to provide a flawless and dignified journey "from pallet to plot"—as Blessing liked to describe it to chance acquaintances at morticians' conventions. *But this mob scene!* Blessing scowled toward the street. What self-respecting, middle-class, bereaved American could be expected to make a favorable judgment on a loved one's behalf after pushing his way through this riffraff of senility?

Blessing sighed and retired to the dark leathers of his office to light a cigar and brood. If the whole mess had never gone beyond that untidy professor, everything might have come out all right. Now, with every toothless crone and rest-home Romeo in town parading out front, the devil only knew what would happen.

By noon—the hour when Blessing chose next to sneak a look outside—the number of demonstrators had grown again. *Thanks to those television bastards.* There must have been thirty or forty of them, he guessed, and the group had gotten rowdier. One yellow little man in a wheelchair caught a glimpse of Blessing and shook a bony fist toward the front door of Eternal Hope. The gesture boded ill.

The real trouble began when the Eternal Hope hearse, returning from the country with the body of Mr. Foster, came gliding down Sycamore Street and drew to a stop before turning into the wide driveway. Blessing had seen it coming, and was already pulling on his gray gloves to assist Saunders and the driver, when he heard the shouts in the street. It sounded like a chant. He listened and could hear the words plainly:

"Here comes the vulture. Here comes the vulture. Here comes the vulture."

Sticks and stones, Blessing thought, but who would have believed all those old farts had so much noise in them? He went about his business, which led him heavily down the back stairs and into the garage. The wide doors were still closed; the hearse was not yet far enough up the drive to trip the electronic door-opener. Blessing temporized, rubbing a stray fingerprint off the chrome window-trim of the second Eternal Hope hearse. It was the older of the two Cadillacs, a haughty, high-silhouetted machine Blessing much preferred to the sleeker model he was now waiting to unload. *Why do we sacrifice dignity for progress?* He rubbed his gloved fingertips together and sighed—his second show of emotion that day—for the slipping away of old virtues.

Minutes, too, were slipping away; the garage remained shut, the enclosed air damp and stale. He retraced his path up the short flight of stairs to the side hall and opened the door to see what was happening; the freshness of a spring wind washed over him as he stepped into the sunlight. The drive was empty. The black limousine had not moved in the street, and the crowd of demonstrators scuffled around it, their voices raised in an untoward clamor, their signboards dancing. Blessing felt rage and fear sweep over him, the back of his neck growing warm, as he trotted clumsily down the driveway.

"Here now," he heard himself saying. "Stop that! Get away from that machine!"

He came to the edge of the mob, his gloved hands raised over his head as if to make some imperious threat. The black hearse, glittering in the sunshine, seemed to be rocking, bouncing on its heavy springs; Blessing felt dizzy from its motion and from the exertion of running. Working his way through the pickets, he could see that groups of old men and women on each side of the limousine were pushing against it, wheezing and laughing: "Heave; heave."

"Stop it, you crazy fools." He had a horrible image of Mr. Foster, inside the van, rattling against the walls, cracking like porcelain if the Cadillac should tip over. *Silly. Impossible.* Then he saw why the car had stopped in the first place: Professor Garvey was lying prostrate on the pavement in front of its massive bumper. "Is nothing sacred?" Blessing screamed.

A face suddenly appeared not six inches from his own—flaccid, twisted with lines the years had made, its eyes milky and gray-lidded. *A perfect Lazarus.* "You fat ghoul," the face said, and spat on him.

Appalled, Blessing ducked and forced his way to the front of the hearse. Through the windshield—was that an egg smashed on the glass, that orange smear dribbling over the wipers?—he could see Saunders, erect and stiff-lipped, and the driver slouched over the wheel with a cigarette in the corner of his mouth; Saunders put up his hand and waved queerly. Breathing hard, feeling his legs aching from his labors, Blessing stooped and seized old Garvey's ankles and hauled him—light as feathers—out of the path of the hearse.

"Go on!" he shouted at Saunders. The assistant opened the window a crack to hear him. "Go on!" Blessing gestured wildly with both arms to illustrate his order. "Get out of here; wait at Memorial Gardens!" he shrieked.

Finally Saunders nodded comprehension. The hearse started to move sluggishly through the protesters, who yelled and cursed and pounded on the roof and sides of the machine with closed fists and the sticks their signs were nailed to.

Blessing stood surprisingly alone and watched the surrounded Cadillac gradually gather speed. A few at a time, the protesters fell behind it; by the time it turned the corner and drove out of sight, the crowd had begun to straggle back to the Eternal Hope.

"It's amazing," said a voice behind him. "It's really exhilarating to see how they've put their hearts into this."

Blessing whirled. It was Garvey, sitting happily on the curbstone, brushing the dust from his trousers.

"You screwy old fossil," Blessing snarled, and hurried across the street to his front door. He could feel his heart pounding, hollow from work and anger, the blood thumping behind his ears, the sweat cooling on his face. He fumbled nervously with the key as he let himself into the front hall, half afraid the crowd would catch him before he could slip inside. The snap of the latch as he shouldered the door closed filled him with relief. And now, surely, he had every right to ask for the intervention of the police. Property had been threatened; the peace had been disturbed. He went to the phone and took in a deep gulp of air to steady his breathing. Then he dialed the mayor.

"This time they've gone too far," he said. He explained the assault on the hearse, the necessity of sending the Eternal Hope Cadillac to a rival mortuary, his unusual labors, the growing unruliness of the crowd outside. "Enough racket to wake the dead," he concluded dramatically.

The voice of the mayor was rich with hesitancy and alternative. Actually the disturbance was minor, the people involved were aged and harmless, probably they would leave by dark; if there was no real damage, perhaps the police should not be involved.

Blessing was stunned. "Real damage; *real* damage!" His voice choked and he slammed the phone into the cradle with disgust.

What is reality? The reputation of Eternal Hope; that was reality. He wondered what the world was coming to, when a city could not be bothered to protect its businessmen.

Yet shortly it appeared that the mayor had had a change of heart, for twenty minutes after Blessing's call the police were at the side door. He had not heard them approaching—there had been no scream of sirens, and no black squad car hurtling across the curb into the midst of the doddering humanity out front. In fact, there were only two men—a lieutenant and a sergeant—and Blessing, who would have wished for a simple but flamboyant display of force to disperse the demonstrators, was disappointed. He had notions, derived from watching riots on television and in the movies, of what repression looked like; it struck him that the mayor was still implying the Eternal Hope was worth precious little expenditure of law and order. He remained annoyed. When he let the two men in, he was too upset to introduce himself or to ask the policemen's names.

"So he finally sent you," was all Blessing said.

The sergeant, who was the younger man, seemed perplexed, but it was the lieutenant who responded. "We volunteered," the officer said.

Now Blessing didn't know what to think of the mayor. "It doesn't matter," he decided. "I'm glad somebody in this town has a little bit of conscience left."

"That's quite a fan club you got out there," the sergeant said, standing at the window to look at the picketers.

"They're no fans of mine," Blessing mumbled unpleasantly. *That mass of unwashed senility.*

The lieutenant already had a notebook opened. "Any damage so far?"

"I can't be sure," Blessing said. "I sent Saunders on to Memorial Gardens—that's a funeral parlor on the other side of town. Competitors. Old-fashioned types." Blessing could not resist sneering. Memorial Gardens hadn't remodeled in thirty years; the place looked like a wedding cake.

"But the car wasn't damaged?" The lieutenant waited to write in his book.

"The limousine," Blessing said. "I can't be certain, the way they were jumping around. They probably dented it. It's a miracle they didn't get at Mr. Foster."

"Who's that?"

"The deceased."

"What did you think they might do to Mr. Foster?"

Blessing pondered. Kidnap him? Bring him back to life? "God knows," he said.

"How did they dent your limousine?"

"With their fists. They were all pounding on the outside of it. They even tried to tip it over." He recalled the terrible vision of poor Mr. Foster rattling around inside the hearse.

The sergeant chortled. "Those old sparrow-bones!" he said. "They couldn't dent Kleenex."

The lieutenant frowned. "What about the building?" he asked Blessing.

"Nothing's smashed yet; but you can imagine what the lawns will look like in the morning."

The lieutenant closed his book and tucked it into his shirt pocket. "We'll see what happens," he said.

"Aren't you going to do anything?"

The lieutenant winked—*Isn't he serious about this?*—at Blessing. "We don't want to be hasty. It's getting on to suppertime; they may get hungry and go on home."

His sergeant, still hovering at the window, seemed to think otherwise. "I don't know," he murmured. "They're the kind that lives on crackers and warm milk. Who'd mind missing a meal like that?"

"Some of them are fasting anyway," Blessing said hopelessly.

"We'll see," the lieutenant said quietly.

The sergeant shrugged. "Why don't you show us around this place?" he said to Blessing.

The request startled him. Yet, though he was reluctant, he was afraid not to cooperate with the police, and so during the next hour Blessing obliged them with a tour such as he usually reserved for visiting high school students and their nervous teachers. The sergeant was especially interested; he asked innocent questions, admired the choice of caskets in the Selection Room, made a nuisance of himself picking up jars and instruments in the laboratory off the garage. He was fascinated by the details of Blessing's lecture—when it was necessary to break the bones of the dead, where the wires were hidden, how the corpses were dressed for eternity. The lieutenant, on the other hand, heard everything in silence and nodded wisely.

At least they looked like riot police; Blessing took some small consolation from the white plastic helmets, the glossy leather jackets—black with enormous silver rivets—and the high, polished boots. Both men carried service revolvers on the left hip, and a small leather case with handcuffs on the right. Both had clubs, thick and wooden, about thirty inches long; the sergeant let his hang from his belt, while the lieutenant held his before him in both hands, as if he were pushing the handle of a wheelbarrow. A special consciousness of authority showed itself in the lieutenant's bearing, as if his rank meant something, as if he truly deserved to be the sergeant's superior. He was older, too—Blessing guessed by ten years—and a quality of restraint and measure was reflected in his movements, his way of talking, the careful concentration of his gaze upon objects in the Eternal Hope rooms. The sergeant was everything his elder was not: brash, a bit loud, with something puppyish in the way he followed the lieutenant about. Blessing felt no hint of discipline in the younger man, and the sergeant's behavior made him edgy. *Irresponsible*—that was the word Blessing settled on. Or perhaps *capricious*. Was that how police departments did things? Put the young with the old, the foolish with the wise? Most likely. And all the pair had in common was the uniform and the weaponry—that in itself the only reassurance to Blessing in his present difficulty with the lively world outside.

"I'd appreciate knowing what it is you plan to do," he said, once they had come back to the reception room and the sergeant had resumed his bemused surveillance from the front window. "It's obvious they won't go away."

He got no answer. The phone rang, and it was Saunders, calling from Memorial Gardens to receive instructions.

"What shall I tell him?" Blessing asked the lieutenant.

"Tell him you'll call him back later."

"And tell Mr. Foster to sit tight," the sergeant put in, delighted with his own wit. "Tell him to wait in the car. And keep his motor running."

Blessing sighed.

The day darkened rapidly. The street lamps on Sycamore glowed and brightened; more and more of the autos of the curious crawled past with headlights turned on. The television truck had taken up a permanent position across the street, and a cameraman crouched precariously on its roof. Blessing paced uneasily from the reception room to the front hall and back again. The two policemen, still helmeted, had dug out of a lower drawer of Blessing's desk a battered Parcheesi board—*Amusing the children is a part of our total service* —and were throwing the dice, manipulating the pieces abstractedly across the lines and boxes. The grandfather's clock in the hall struck a somber seven o'clock. Outside, the sound of ancient voices rose and fell like a ritual chorus against the walls of Eternal Hope.

"You know," the brash sergeant said to Blessing, "I bet your buddies over at that Memorial Gardens place are fit to be tied. Jealous. You standing here with all those overripe bodies stampeding your front porch."

"That's not the way I see it," Blessing said coldly. What he *did* see was the absurdity of the position he was in. Since he couldn't declare a moratorium on death, what could he do? These two casual officers of the law were his only hope. He watched them, throwing the white dice in turn, moving counters as if nothing depended on the moves; what did they care for the problems of Thomas Blessing? Their disinterest galled him.

"The damned fools won't leave," he said. He intended to sound impatient.

The lieutenant brought his leg down from the arm of the chair he sat in; the sergeant began to put the game away.

"And they're getting louder," Blessing said.

The lieutenant rose ponderously to his feet. "Do you have any sort of outside lighting?" he asked.

Blessing nodded. "Baby floods. We have a half-dozen across the front of the building." *A Beacon for the Bereaved*; it was a motto he had thought of—had even wanted to include in the Eternal Hope letterhead.

"Turn them on," the lieutenant said.

The switch was beside the front door, and Blessing pushed it downward through its silent mercurial arc. Light blossomed on the other side of the door and flowed through the side curtains into the hall. He peered through the curtains. Tonight he could see clearly the signs the pickets carried: *Give Us Back Old Friends; Heaven, No, We Won't Go; No*—Garvey, Laurence Garvey, the professorial bag of bones that had started everything, standing in the forefront of this decrepit rabble.

"I'll talk to them," the lieutenant said. He pulled open the door and stepped outside. A chorus of hissing and booing greeted him; he held up his hands, the slender wooden club still connecting his two fists. The aged crowd quieted and he confronted them while the glare of the lights sparkled from his jacket rivets and his helmet. More floodlighting—from the television unit on the other side of the protesters—bathed the lieutenant. *Imagine the size of his shadow.*

"I'm not here to make a speech," the lieutenant said. A murmur rose and fell away before him. "I only want to say a few words to you. I want to say that this funeral home is a place of business, legally incorporated under the law. It conducts its business according to the same law. You—all of you—are interfering with the proper business of this funeral home. You stand in violation of the law, and you are all liable to punishment for breaking it."

Blessing, behind the half-opened door, watched the mob on his ruined lawn, the mob wedged through his precious barberry hedge, the mob supported upon canes and crutches and glittering wheelchairs. He studied the lined faces, the bald skulls, the gaping, toothless mouths of men and women who were both his curse and his livelihood. They frightened him; he felt the desire to embrace them; he imagined their cadaverous flesh laid out to be beautified in the cellars of Eternal Hope. He heard their voices mocking the lieutenant, and saw their yellowed fists lifted against him.

The lieutenant went on: "We don't want to hurt you. I ask you—

I plead with you—Go home; stop this pointless demonstration. The death you think you're defying cannot be defied. You have nothing to gain by your actions."

Blessing found himself nodding his head. The sergeant, beside him, subdued as Blessing had not seen him subdued, said softly: "He's good, isn't he? He's not just any goddamned cop."

The lieutenant was finishing. "I ask you—please—to go away. You have five minutes. After five minutes, you will be forced to disperse. Talk it over among yourselves. Be reasonable. Think of the consequences."

When the lieutenant came inside his expression was solemn, and he shook his head regretfully. "I wish they were younger," he told Blessing. "The old ones, they think they have nothing to lose. I don't like it."

The sergeant seized his arm. "You were terrific," he said.

"Let's wait a while," said the lieutenant.

For his own part, Blessing was keyed up, as if for the first time his prayers were being answered, and in the excitement of the moment of ultimatum he forgot his earlier bitterness toward the mayor and the police. Now he saw that the end of his problems was imminent—that for better or worse the crowd would clear his lawns and unblock his door. He was half beside himself with the waiting. He ran from window to window, watching and talking to himself, trying to guess which old man or woman would be first to drift away from the crowd. He was even on the verge of putting in a phone call to Saunders, commanding him back to Eternal Hope with Mr. Foster, when he heard the smashing of glass from the direction of the side lawn. Under a window of the reception room he picked up the missile—an empty Geritol bottle. Clearly, the demonstrators would not disperse; instead, they had turned violent.

The five minutes expired. In the hall of Eternal Hope the two policemen conferred briefly. The sergeant had taken the club from his belt; he listened with respect to his superior.

"You needn't hit hard," Blessing heard the lieutenant say. "You needn't hit more than once. These are old men and old women, and they aren't strong, and they aren't going to fight back. Now use your common sense; don't try to beat up on all of them. One in five, one in ten—that's enough. The rest will run."

The sergeant nodded; he nudged Blessing's arm. "You watch this," he said, and followed the lieutenant outside.

Relief, horror, satisfaction, remorse, rage, mercy—all of these mingled in the breast of Thomas Blessing as he watched the two policemen enter the crowd. In their black uniforms and dazzling headpieces they looked larger than life. They moved slowly and methodically among the old men and women, their pale, polished clubs held high in their right fists, their left arms straight before them to fend off the angry pickets. The clubs fell downward in wide, swift arcs—first upon Laurence Garvey, whose terse signboard fluttered into the air above his head; upon the little yellow woman in the wheelchair; upon the white-haired woman with the crippled foot; upon one after another of these loose-skinned, desperate adversaries of death. Upon each victim the officers exercised a single graceful stroke, and when each was struck he toppled—silent, slow, like an object in a dream; and where each fell, he lay without moving.

On the Island

On the first Sunday in September there was a storm, and the following morning the carcass of a seal washed up on the short, sandy beach below Minot Point. When the Kennett boys found it—and ran back to the house telling about it—it was shapeless and bloated, a pale, puffed-up sac of poisons rolling and tumbling in the yellow water. Someone had shot it; a small hole, clean and bloodless, showed above its tiny, glazed eyes. It had been dead for a week, said one of the boys. No, said the other, older boy, only three or four days; there was no stench of decay to drive you back from the beach.

By midmorning all of Pine Cove had been told. Some of the men and most of the children came down to the water's edge and stood in a ragged half-circle around the swollen flesh—not mourning, any of them, but still and respectful. A few gulls, black against the sun but silver circling away, called nervously over the heads of the people as over a picnic.

Long before dusk only the children remained on the beach, and most of them were boys. They squatted on the sand and sat on the black rocks and made a chorus with the rising and falling water. As the seal rolled up the beach, their voices pitched upward in unison; as it lolled back, their voices trailed downward. Over and over they sang the senseless dirge; it was like slow wind in the sparse pines that stood above the point. Old lobstermen who had long ago given up hauling traps heard the treble chant, and they shuddered without knowing why.

Lyle Kennett heard it and lifted his hands to his ears to shut out the sound. It was a slow movement of some delicacy, for he was an old man in pain who passed the long afternoons in motionless remembering, seated on an open porch overlooking the sea. What remained of his world lay eastward; it included the narrow channel of green water separating the mainland from Needle Island, the island itself with its overgrowth of hightopped pines and evergreen scrub, and, in transparent weather, the remote low shadow of Monhegan beyond the southern and most slender tip of the Needle.

Often Lyle noticed activity on the island, for several years earlier a man from a city had built a small brick cottage on the weather side where the strip of ledge and sand was broadest. The cottage was half-hidden, but in the evening stubs of short firs stood out in silhouette against lighted windows. When the breeze was onshore Lyle heard the closing of doors and, rarely, the murmur of voices. The builder's eldest son spent vacation summers on the island. Lyle had never seen him; he knew only that the young man owned a rifle, for day after day the noise of sharp firing reached him across the channel. It was the gravest and loudest of all interruptions, and was by itself the reason that Lyle had asked no more than the first question when Martha, his son's wife, came out of the kitchen after putting away the noon dishes.

"What's that devilish whining?" he had said, lowering his thin hands to his lap.

"The children," she answered. "There's a seal dead, down on the beach."

"I should go down there," he said.

Lyle had never heard such a sound. Now, trying to think above the voices of the children, he could not have said how many days had passed since he last saw seals on the gray layers of rock at the end of the Needle and in the dark water at the channel's mouth, but he knew he had missed them in the way men miss all easy pleasures. There were many seals in the cove—Lyle had seen nine and ten at once—and their antics were the single delight of his inactive days. They wriggled ponderously over the rocks, rolling and toppling one another into the sea; once in the water they vanished beneath the choppy surface, then reappeared a hundred feet away, their slick snouts and gray heads bobbing foolishly into the light.

When he was much younger and taking a charter fishing party out of Pine Cove, Lyle thought he had seen a rare white seal sunning itself on a ledge; the next day he saw it again, but when he steered close to shore he discovered only the outline of a seal made with whitewash on an upright face of rock. The matter-of-fact seals in the cove provoked that memory; he told stories about the white seal, but he had never told the truth. All his life the fact had seemed less important than the wonderful pretense.

Abruptly, the unison voices stopped. A few minutes later the children—Lyle's two grandsons among them—appeared on the ridge overlooking the beach. They turned away from the Kennett house and ran laughing, under shadow, in the grove of pines. When he could no longer see them, Lyle stood up and shuffled unsteadily across the porch. As he started fumbling along the pipe-iron railing beside the steps, Martha came to the door.

"Where are you going now?"

"Down to see for myself," he said.

"Supper's in a half-hour," she said, "and be careful climbing down that hill."

He reached the foot of the steps and began walking deliberately toward the ridge. Without looking around he was aware of Martha watching him with embarrassing concern, and he made an impatient, backward gesture with his hand. He was pleased to hear the screen door of the kitchen swing shut.

Lyle went stiffly down the narrow footpath toward the sea, where left and right beside the path were small white wildflowers trampled under the dry stalks of grass by children's feet. The dirt path wound through the grass, around and among gray rocks sparkling pink with mica in the rays of the late sun. At intervals its course was broken by ledges of roots and pebbles, and at these interruptions the old man stepped slowly, reaching to the earth for support, so that his journey was like that of a man descending a rotten staircase. In time the path gave way to a waste of black scrub and flat black stones swept smooth by tides; here Lyle stopped for a moment resting with his hands on his hips, at the head of the beach.

The dead hulk of the seal lay echoing with the throb of the water; the dark sand was wet and clean around it. Approaching the carcass, Lyle knew what had driven the children away. Tired of the game of their voices, they had gathered stones and sticks from the beach and hillside, and then, circling the seal like dancers, they had pelted it with the stones and poked at it with the sticks. Out of a score of gashes and tears had burst the stench and corrupt matter of decay, repelling the celebrants in a scurry of astonished cries. They would not come back. Some of the stones were still embedded in the dead creature's flesh; nearby, two or three short driftwood sticks turned in the shallow water.

The stench was powerful; it caught in Lyle's throat and woke a sharp agony below his chest. He stepped back and away. Then he moved across the beach and stood, looking at the seal, with his hands in the pockets of his overalls. He thought it was like standing over an open grave.

The sun by now was behind the grove of pines on the hill, and the shade was cold on the back of Lyle's neck. As he turned, intending to climb back up the path to the house, he saw two men coming down the slope toward him.

"What you doing, Lyle? Saying a prayer on the poor bugger?"

Squinting, he recognized Chris Simpson, a near neighbor and one of the cove's councilmen. The man following wore a uniform; Lyle did not know him.

"She's starting to stink," Lyle said. "The kids poked holes in her hide."

Simpson walked past him, halted, and came back holding his nose. "Makes a man want to puke," he said. "This is Daniels, warden over from Damariscotta. Lyle Kennett."

Lyle shook hands. The game warden was a young man, his face smooth and tanned, and he wore his uniform stiffly.

"Somebody shot her," Lyle said.

"I don't suppose there's any way to find out who it was," Daniels mused. "You people swim off this beach?"

"Kids do, some," Simpson told him. "We ought to get rid of this thing soon as we can."

"Won't be no more seals in the cove till we do," Lyle said. He watched the young man closely. "Might be they'll never come back at all."

Daniels was studying the dead seal, scratching his nose. Simpson scuffed his feet in the sand as if he were impatient. Finally the young warden coughed and made a clucking noise with his tongue.

"I don't suppose there's much chance it'd burn," he said, "all waterlogged like it is."

"We could bury it," Simpson suggested.

"She don't belong ashore," Lyle said. "I could take her out to sea."

"You let the State of Maine worry about disposing of this mess," Daniels said briskly. "That's not a bad idea, though," he added. "You got a boat?"

"I got one," Simpson said, "with a good little five-horse outboard. Wouldn't take me ten minutes to fetch her around."

"Of course I got a boat," Lyle said peevishly.

"You go get yours," the game warden told Simpson. "Bring some rope and we'll clean off this beach before dark."

"You bet," Simpson said. "Won't take me ten minutes."

Lyle watched the man scramble up the embankment to the road. Left alone with Daniels, he felt more strongly a personal irritation at the young man's way.

"What do you figure on doing?" he asked.

"Tow it out and cut it loose," Daniels said. "Simple as that."

"She'll come back."

"Not if we tow it far enough."

"How far?"

"Three, maybe four miles out."

Lyle shook his head. "She'll come back on the next tide, or the next one after that."

"We'll wait and see," said the young man.

When Simpson arrived with his boat, a shiny aluminum skiff powered by a new outboard, the two men had been standing silently for a quarter of an hour. Lyle stood back from the shore and watched them go about their work, the warden tying a wet handkerchief over his nose and mouth before he waded into the water to wind several lengths of line around the bloated seal. Daniels was scrupulously careful not to touch the creature more than he had to in binding it, and he took pains to carry easy extra loops around the seal's useless flippers. When he had finished, he secured one end of the line in a slipknot and threw the other end into the boat. During this performance Simpson knelt in the beached skiff, holding tightly to the sides and looking off in the direction of the ocean horizon. As he made the line fast to a seat, his lips were compressed and colorless.

At last they were ready. Daniels pushed the skiff into deeper water and vaulted aboard. Simpson lowered the screw of the outboard and yanked life into it. Then the skiff edged away from the shore, Simpson steering, Daniels holding out the rope to keep it from fouling. The rope tightened; the great dead beast slid noiselessly into the small surf and followed the silver skiff away from the beach.

For nearly twenty minutes Lyle traced the progress of Simpson's boat, seeing Daniels remove the handkerchief and drop it over the side, Simpson move his head as though he were talking at last. Once they had cleared the tip of Needle Island they held to a southeasterly course. Before long Lyle could not see the men, only the metal boat shining on the sea and the dun-colored seal bobbing behind it in the choppy water. The tide was running toward the full, and when Lyle looked down at his feet the dark traces of the seal's track had been softened by the waves and nearly obliterated.

When he returned to the house, Martha had put supper on the table. He sat at his place—the eldest grandson to the left of him, the youngest at the right—bowing his head not for grace but to recover his breath after the climb from the beach. When he looked up he met the questioning of his son's eyes from across the table. Lyle managed a gray smile.

"Frank," he said faintly, "the old man's a little winded."

"You quit running up and down that hill," Frank said. "That's plain foolish at your age."

"He went down to look at that poor seal," Martha said. She set bowls of chowder around the table and sat down beside her husband. "Isn't anybody going to do anything about it? It's going to start smelling up the whole cove."

"Chris and some game warden dragged her off," Lyle said. "They think that's the end of it."

"Oh, sure it is," said Frank. "It'll go straight to the bottom."

"They never bothered to weigh her down."

Frank showed surprise, the spoon halted for an instant before his opened mouth. He finished the motion and swallowed. "That's a dumb thing," he said. "They could have got an old anchor down at the landing."

"They didn't," Lyle said. "She'll come back with the tides."

"Who shot it, Gramps?" asked the oldest boy.

"I don't know."

Frank coughed contemptuously. "The hell you don't."

"Frank."

He glanced from his wife to his two sons and went on:

"I didn't tell you what happened this morning. Lou Keeley and me took his boat out past the Needle just before noon, and you know what I fished out of the water near that red channel buoy? A big cormorant with his silly head shot half off."

Martha put both hands to her face. "Oh, my," she said.

"You know how they perch on top of the marker," Frank said. "The kid must have picked it off for the fun of it."

"No sense to it," Lyle agreed.

"He's wild, and that's not the first dead thing I've seen floating in the channel. Gulls, lots of times. The seal's the biggest thing he's killed yet. One of these days he'll get himself a man, and then the cove'll wake up."

"He wouldn't ever shoot a man, would he?" said the youngest boy.

Frank shrugged. "It wouldn't surprise me."

"You've seen him?" Lyle asked.

"He hangs around the landing, nights. Always wears a black sweatshirt with a hood on it—name of some college on his chest. He never talks, and I never heard anybody talk to him."

"Queer," said Martha.

"He's got that power boat of his father's," said Frank. "That big mahogany-looking thirty-footer."

"I've never noticed it," Lyle said.

"He never goes near it, that's why. You'd think he'd spend his time fishing from it if he's so damned bored on the island. He could run out ten or fifteen miles past Monhegan and drift all day. There's fish out there, too."

Frank wiped his mouth with his palm and pushed his chair back from the table. As he stood up, he gave his wife a hard slap on the rump. "Good chowder," he said.

Lyle went on eating in silence; he found the chowder tasteless. "I think I'll go to bed early," he said, getting up from the table.

"Sleep late tomorrow," Martha said. The embarrassing concern was still in her voice. "You look peaked."

"Good night," he said.

Inside his room at the top of the back stairs, Lyle undressed slowly and got into bed without turning on the lamp. Some little of the diminishing daylight still discovered the objects around him. At the foot of his narrow bed was the antique cupboard where maps were stored; along one wall stood the high chifforobe, and on it a pewter pitcher and metal washbasin; under the window by the bed was the black captain's chair with its burden of clothing. There was little else to be seen. Hidden beneath the bed was the heavy porcelain vessel which Lyle used at night, and which Martha emptied—grumbling—in the morning. The bedroom was small and personal, secure and private.

Lyle did not immediately close his eyes, nor had he intended to when he left the kitchen. He could not remember how many months had gone by since he had last known a genuine desire for sleep. Even when he was most tired—and he realized as he lay looking about the darkening room that he had never before in his life been so exhausted—sleep no longer attracted him. Each night was a conflict not resolved; he feared that he might not again open his eyes to see day, and then—after he had chided himself for an old man's fool cowardice—the assurance that he would indeed awaken to many more mornings yet unthought about struck with a special terror.

This evening, he found himself thinking about the nameless young man on the island, and he sought aimlessly after reasons for the actions of youth. He discovered none, not knowing if there were no reasons, or if they were only remote from his weak scrutiny. Lyle could no more comprehend the killing of poor sea creatures than he could understand his own struggles with sleep.

He lay still, hearing the sea below his window, the light breeze rustling through the curtains, the faraway clatter of supper dishes downstairs. All in a moment, he thought of tomorrow, of the seal coming back, and a feeling of elation seized him that put all panic and dullness from his mind. The final passing of twilight from his tiny room he did not notice. He was suddenly light-headed, and he slipped at once through giddiness into the drowsy beginnings of a dream.

He did not wake until shortly past noon. Then, he dressed himself in the clothes he had taken off the night before; downstairs, he poured and swallowed with a bitter face a cup of black coffee from the pot at the back of the kitchen stove, and went out to look at his half-world of water and horizon. The elation had not left him, but it was only in the clarity of day seen from the small porch that he sensed its vast influence.

What he saw, he had never seen. His eyes played incredible tricks with colors of the familiar: the calm channel was chalk-orange, the sea outside the cove a broad, swelling meadow of dull gold; the scrub fir and thin pines of the Needle had turned to hollow red as if they were the valleys and peaks of fire caught in one instant of burning, and the sky took up the strange hues of the earth in a pale wash of pink the color of turning petals. Far off, the tiny fin of a sail glided black over the copper waves, and the small cottage on the island appeared in an angular disguise of innocent blue.

Lyle faltered and stumbled to his chair. He was dizzy and disturbed. None of what he now saw stood still, but shimmered and warped as if he were perceiving this grotesque world from the near side of a wall of immense heat. Objects grew and wasted, in and out of focus, each in its turn as a disconnected image. When he closed his eyes, the brightness of his lids was dazzling; his ears rang with a shrill whine he could not identify. "I'm daft," he thought. He uttered the word "daft" louder than he had intended, and the echo of it came back from the barrier of the island as a high, unintelligible syllable. Then the hallucination passed as suddenly as it had seized him, and he sat overlooking his ordinary view, enervated, and cold with sweating.

All afternoon he waited for someone to come and tell him about the seal. He dared not purposely think of its returning; yet his mind accepted thoughts of nothing else. Anticipation haunted him, and hope hovered impatiently in the bright day that floated away on slow currents of light. When the sun had set, and the first gray mists blurred the horizon line, Lyle closed his eyes and clasped his hands into a figure of resignation. When he opened his eyes, the youngest boy was standing at the foot of the porch steps, looking up at him.

"It came back," the boy said.

Lyle parted his hands and smiled at the boy. "Where?" he asked.

"In just the same place as before—the way you said."

"You run along," said Lyle. He raised himself from the chair. "Just run along."

"What are you going to do?"

"Take a little walk," said Lyle. "A little look-see."

The boy backed away. "It's all covered over with ropes," he said, and ran up the path out of sight.

Walking as quickly as he was able, Lyle went to the ridge and peered down toward the beach. The seal, still ropebound, was a dark shadow in the twilit water close to shore; where the incoming tide encircled it, a triangle of dry sand pointed away from it to the higher land. As Lyle watched, Chris Simpson came up beside him. The two men stood quietly, Simpson chewing on a cold pipe and shuffling his feet.

"Won't Daniels raise Cain," Simpson said at last.

"I told him," said Lyle. "He ought to've listened."

"When he gets back from Damariscotta, he'll have to start all over again." Simpson snickered. "I guess this time I'll rent him my boat."

"No need. I'll take care of her."

"What for?"

"I should've done it in the first place."

Simpson hesitated. "You ought at least to get his permission."

"Then he'd best give me it right now," Lyle said. "I'm going to take her off tonight."

"I told you: Daniels is in Damariscotta. He won't be back till morning."

"I can't wait."

"Then I'm damned if I know what to say to you." Simpson whacked the bowl of the pipe against his heel. He tucked the pipe-stem into the corner of his mouth and scowled at Lyle. "You're a stubborn so-and-so," he said; the words whistled between his clenched teeth.

"I know how much stink I can stand," Lyle said, "and how much I can't."

Simpson gave the problem long consideration. "I won't stop you," he said finally. "I won't lift a finger to help you, neither, but I won't hinder you." He began walking away.

"I don't know if I can do it alone." Lyle said after him.

"That's your lookout," Simpson answered.

Lyle saw him go, then retraced his steps to the house. The kitchen was lighted, and the family seated around the table. Martha studied him as he entered, her gaze sharp and—he thought—more troubled than ever.

"Don't wash up," she said. "Your food's already cold."

"I'm not hungry," Lyle told her, "so I think I'll go upstairs."

"You didn't eat a thing all day," she said, her eyes still piercing him. "I left your lunch in the icebox, and you never even touched it."

"What's the matter?" asked Frank.

"I'll sit and talk," Lyle said, "but I'm not hungry." He took his place at the table and grinned foolishly at Frank. "The seal came back," he said.

Frank shook his head. "I'd like to know what's so interesting about that damned seal."

Lyle searched for a safe answer. "It gives a man something to think about."

"Waste of time," said Frank with his mouth full. He swallowed.

"You know what that crazy kid did today?—early this morning, I guess. Went and shot up Lou's lobster buoys, those quart ale bottles he uses. How's that for a joke?"

"Poor Lou," Martha said.

"Poor Frank," Frank said. "I told him I'd help him drag for his traps tomorrow forenoon, and that's my time wasted. I'd like to tangle with that dumb sharpshooter, I'll tell you."

"That's not a good idea for you," Lyle said.

"It'd be a pleasure." Frank stopped, his knife suspended over his plate. "I'll have to put off driving you in to Doc Corbett's till day after tomorrow. I promised Lou."

"That's all right."

"You feel okay?"

"Pretty good," said Lyle, "today."

"But take it easy, will you?"

"I don't do a thing but sit," Lyle said.

"That's all you need to do," said Frank.

Lyle stood up. "You finish," he said. "I'll go upstairs and get some rest." He halted in the doorway and turned to Martha. "Wait breakfast tomorrow; I think I'll start getting up early again."

In his room, Lyle sat heavily on the edge of the bed and awaited the passage of time. He expected Martha to climb the stairs and insist that he drink some broth or a glass of milk, but she remained below. He considered getting out his maps and charts and spreading them across the bed to look up the familiar names of islands and reefs; he even thought about switching on the light and sewing a button he had lost from the cuff of his shirt. He did neither, but listened to the voices beneath his room as he waited in darkness. So much seemed now unimportant that he could not regret doing nothing. Changing his clothes, eating lunch, explaining to Chris Simpson and Frank his feeling for the seal—all were submerged in the same strange joy which the youngest boy had revived with the words: "It came back."

He sat in the dark for hours. It was not until he was sure that Martha and Frank were in bed asleep that he descended the back stairs, carefully, groping down the length of the slender railing with both his hands. He went across the kitchen, out the porch door, and into the cool night with its minor conflict of waves and crickets. The moon was rising, and barely lit his way to the narrow dock below the house.

His boat—an old, weathered dory that cast a bulky shadow on the water—was moored at the end of the dock. It swung sedately with the channel currents, its high bow bumping against the wharf edge, and Lyle made three trips to it from the land end of the dock. He put aboard the oars, then a dirty coil of rope. Finally, from under the dock, he dragged out two rust-covered pieces of ballast lead; he guessed their combined weight at something over a hundred pounds, and he lowered them with awkward slowness into the dory. This done, Lyle took a last look around him, as though he were cataloguing not only the contents of the boat, but all the objects and sounds of the cove; then he stepped aboard, cast off, and began rowing the few hundred feet to the beach where the seal lay.

It was midnight when Lyle reached the inlet. The moon was hidden by cloud, but a weak, phosphor glow rose from the muted sea and cast pale blue reflections all around him. The edge of the narrow beach was brilliant where the small waves burst and slid shell-shapes of light over the level shelf of sand. Above the shore, the hill and the shabby grove of pines were dim pretensions to reality. No sound reached him here but the slap of his oars and the restless noise of the ocean.

Close to land, when he felt the keel crunch across pebbles, Lyle shipped the oars and squirmed out of the boat into shallow water. Calf-deep in the sea, he pulled the dory as far up on the beach as he could manage. The action winded him, and he paused for several minutes, leaning against the boat to rest.

The outline of the rotting seal was vivid at the water's edge, a few yards to his left. No one had moved it; with the nudge of every wave it glimmered in the false light like an absurd gelatin. It appeared larger now than Lyle had remembered, but he began. He began by undoing what Daniels had done, throwing off the loose cords which crossed and recrossed the seal's bulk, until he had laid the creature bare and ready for his own rope. He knelt and pushed the first strand of his line under the seal, drawing out his arm wet with sand and decay.

Sweating, trembling, choking on the foul air of another world, Lyle worked for an hour to prepare the soft carcass for burial. The labor of it sickened him and insulted his senses; his muscles shuddered with wave upon wave of nausea; his lungs burned from the friction of each false breathing movement; his eyelids turned raw and stung with tears. Everywhere, his fingers operated stiffly over wet layers of flesh that ruptured and peeled at a touch; the feel of the cold skin was like the backwater slime, running and soft, of stagnant sea-grasses. When he was forced to stop and turn his back, desperate for a clean breath, Lyle heard behind him—or was it imagination?—the ghostly sigh of the seal endlessly dying; it was a sound like thousands of tiny mouths of foam opening out of the tide with a continuous hiss that had nothing to do with mortality. Once, he spun around with an angry curse to provoke the huge creature into a single last living movement, but no part of the beast responded: when Lyle fell off balance his hand plunged to the wrist in a swamp of dead matter, and when he tightened the last length of rope into a knot below the seal's small head, the cord cut down through flesh until it drew tight around invisible bone.

Lyle had not imagined the weight of the carcass, and the effort of half-carrying, half-dragging it to the dory and tumbling it into the stern was excessive for him. His hands and arms trembled from cold and fatigue; his clothes—the front of his shirt and overalls and the tops of his shoes—were stained from contact with the seal. By now, his senses were caught at a pitch of sensitivity amounting to numbness.

Numbed, too, were his perceptions of time and space, with the result that from the time he pushed off from the beach and hauled himself into the dory, all the minutes of the early morning crowded close against one another in his mind, and all distance seemed none. He rowed for hours without knowing how long or how far, his back bowing and coming erect in the rhythm of his work, his feet buried and wet in the corpse before him. He only guessed when he was beyond the onshore currents, in water deep enough for his purpose.

Then he put aside the oars to let his boat drift on the pale sea; he attached weights to ropes with careful knots, and plucked at the wound cords with testing fingers which reassured him.

Near daylight, Lyle wrestled the lead and the burden of the seal over the side of the dory. He saw the carcass sink, carried down by the stubborn weights, leaving a surface trail of yellow, hissing foam and fat bubbles of putrid air. For a few moments he knelt resting in the bottom of the boat, drawing in deep breaths. He did not watch the last traces of the animal disappear on the water; it could not even be said that he felt satisfaction with what he had done. When he was rested, he gripped the oars and rowed shoreward.

The dawn was a memorable red, that sort of vivid announcement of day which is like a burst of blood over the horizon, nothing about it faint or timid. It was a glorious warning of heat and a merciless sun. It turned the eastern sea scarlet, and Monhegan Island stood out of the water to the northeast, looking the color of rust. Lyle kept the sunrise before him as he rowed, his back to the land, thinking of nothing. The small crests of the ocean slapped against the boat; the trailing path of slick water spun itself into filaments of green and white froth; the tiny black whirlpools from the oar blades were swept by the hundreds out of sight in the tide. Lyle rowed mechanically, feeling the sharp pain of his unusual labor in the muscles of his shoulders and belly.

He had reached the southern tip of Needle Island, only two hundred yards from the mainland, when he heard one rifle shot, and then another. Startled, he shipped the oars and drifted closer. At the sound of the shots, a colony of gulls had cried up from the dark rocks, looking like streaks of spray in the sunlight. Their bright wings carried them upward in protesting spirals, in and out of shadow; their clamor as they circled above the dory was like children's voices.

When the side of the boat bumped on the rocky shore of the Needle, Lyle stepped over to dry land, leaving the dory to bob unmoored behind him, knowing that it would drift away into the slow currents of the channel. Before him was a barrier of scrub pine and yellow brush, and behind that wall—in one instant singled out from all the rest—he heard the four-syllabled sound of a rifle bolt opened and closed. Wearily, he started toward it, his face hot with the dawn· and his eyes dazzled by the low, red sun. What now moved his aching legs was little more than the same durable elation which had sustained him through his first thirty-six hours of death.

Others

At first the word is a passion in Philip's mind. It cries out in fevered images in the shadows of rooms. It glitters in the delirium of rain on dark window panes. It allies itself with voices and drinking and difficult movement from place to place. It is incessant.

Though it is only a word it has become, with time, so real that Philip often sits, as now, in an attitude suggesting pain, with his eyes shut and his hands over his ears. This is an absurd pose for him to strike in the tiny room of a German hotel at midnight; the silence is almost absolute, and he is not even alone.

He tries to relax. He puts his hands away from his head, and opens his eyes. The word goes away. He lights a cigarette. He sees Cathy, his wife, lying in bed against a pair of pillows, reading a magazine. She has pulled the quilted comforter over her knees; a pale blue sweater is arranged across her shoulders. As if his glance were an abrupt, physical touch, she looks up.

"What is it?" she says. The bedside lamp lights one side of her face and shades the other. She is half smiling.

"It just happened again," he tells her. "I must be worn out."

"Maybe you're not used to being on land. They say that bothers people right after a crossing."

"I guess that's it."

"Sally told me she was land-sick." The single corner of her smile turned upward: "Isn't that just like Sally?"

"Just." Sally is one of the others.

"You ought to get some sleep."

Philip stands up. "I think I will."

He goes to the wash basin and runs water on the cigarette butt. He drops it into the wastebasket and begins to undress. He thinks it is true that he does not feel well; his throat aches and an odd languor informs his arms and legs. He suspects he may be running a temperature.

"This room is like an ice-box," his wife says.

"I told the others we should have waited until April."

"But then you'd have had to leave me home."

Philip sits, naked, on the edge of the bed. "I forgot," he says, truthfully. "Is everything all right?"

"You know I've been fine since the fourth month," she says.

"I'm showing concern," he answers. He leans across the bed to kiss her. She lets the magazine fall and clings to him with a familiar compulsiveness. He draws away too soon.

"What's the matter?"

"I feel rotten," he says. He sits shivering beside her. "Really rotten."

"You get under the covers." She arranges the pillows and moves nearer the light to make room. "You're like ice."

Philip lies next to her under the heavy puff, stretching out his legs and hugging the warm pillow. He stops trembling. He tries to think what he will do if he is genuinely sick in the morning. He pictures the disgust of the others: Damon, Jenny, Chris, Sally. They will condemn his weakness when there is still travel ahead of them. They will damn him; he dares not be in poor health.

"Phil?"

"I'm fine," he says.

"Phil, don't be that way. Don't feel obliged to be sympathetic with me, just because I'm pregnant."

"I don't feel obliged."

"I wish you wouldn't force yourself," she insists. "I know you resent the idea, but don't force yourself not to."

He puts out his hand to touch her—her throat, her small breasts, the full, hard mound of her belly. "I don't resent anything," he says, "only I don't know what to expect."

"We'll know in a month." She rests her hand on his, stroking his fingers gently. "I'm sure it's going to be a boy. I dream about little boys, and you know how strong the heartbeat is. Masculine strength."

"Spare me," Philip says. She often misunderstands.

"Poor Phil." She raises her head from the pillow and kisses his eyelids. "Your cheeks are so flushed, dearest."

"I'll be better in the morning."

"Please do be," she says. She releases his hand and turns out the light.

Philip lies on his stomach and tries to think of nothing. He makes himself acutely sensitive to his surroundings—the movements of his wife as she settles down to rest, the echo of his own heart at his temples, the rattle of the March rain at the windows. He is wide awake, but he does not think.

"Phil," says his wife, and her voice is barely audible above the weather, "when you talk about what to expect, that isn't what you mean, is it? Not the things I say to you."

"Not exactly."

"Boy or girl doesn't matter."

"I don't think so."

"I'm sorry, Phil."

"For God's sake, Cathy!"

He is exasperated, and pushed into thinking. It is like her to apologize for chance. It is like her to plead guilt for every misfortune. It has been like her, from the moment of their vows, to assume all responsibilities and make room for them in the honeycomb of her conscience. She seizes the blame for poems he lacks patience to finish, teaching jobs he cannot hold, fellowships he always loses. His mind rummages through her perverse martyrdoms. Now, and for the rest of her life, she will have the baby as a burden endlessly to be forgiven her. Forever and ever she will be a falsetto saint. It is an image impossible to dwell on.

He pulls himself upright in bed and hammers the pillow with his fist.

"Are you all right, Phil?"

"Hell, yes, I'm in the pink." It is too late to prevent the reflex of his voice. "I'm in rare good health." Then he feels her hand touch his cheek with a delicacy that shames him. "It's all right," he says, "only it's hard to get to sleep."

Her fingers move to his brow and caress his temples. "It doesn't feel as if you have a temperature."

"No." He is impatient. "Come on; get some rest."

She withdraws her hand and lies quietly. Philip feels better, calmer, like the thrum of the rain.

"Please don't go to sleep in a mood, Phil. Be jolly."

"Get some rest," he says. "Remember, you're sleeping for two." It is absurd to be jolly.

"Phil." She giggles like a child. "What a silly thing."

Soon after he has said it, she is asleep. For the rest of the night the very presence of his wife close by him, breathing evenly, nags at his peace.

He gets out of bed at noon, feeling light-headed and unrefreshed. He dresses and smokes a cigarette, sitting wearily by a window where he can look out on the streets. He hears Cathy get up, wash, rustle about the room in her nightgown.

"It's chilly," she says.

He does not look around. He takes no pleasure from seeing his wife dress, though once this was ritual with him. He believes she is ashamed of her ripeness, and he thinks he is more offended by her shame than by her body.

"Shall I pack your briefcase?" she asks.

"No. I'm going to try and work."

She leaves the room. Philip pushes open the window, takes a last drag from his cigarette and tosses it into the street. The view is barren. Across the gray cobbles is a broad meadow filled with buildings caved into their foundations; further off stands the Gothic spire of a gutted church, spindly gulls wheeling about it; the sky is drab. Philip finds paper and pencil and sits studying the church. He writes nothing. He has not written anything for seven months; everything eludes him. He is grateful for a knocking at the door.

"It's Chris," says a voice. Chris comes in, carrying a bottle of beer.

A grotesque, bearded man with skinny hands.

"What's on?" Philip says.

"Party." Chris sprawls on the bed and sets the bottle on the floor. "The *Berlin* sails at two-thirty, and Damon got visitor's passes last night from a seaman. You coming?"

"Damon going to be there?"

"It's his party."

Philip nods: it is all Damon's party. "What about the train?"

"Ten tonight. Twenty-two hours, the Krauts say." He picks up the bottle and gulps from it, spilling. "You working?"

"Trying to, but not."

"You should have gone out with us. We've just been back here a couple of hours."

"I was bushed," Philip says.

"This town's full of bars and whores. I could retire here and expatriate my brains out."

"Are we going to Switzerland?"

"Damon says. We change trains in Bremen and Basel."

"Then?"

Chris sucks at the neck of the bottle and shrugs. "I guess Rome. Damon's got friends there. Maybe I'll get to the Vatican."

Cathy comes in quietly. She greets Chris with what starts as a smile, then turns to dislike at one corner of her mouth.

"Kate the mate," Chris says loudly. "You look more obscene every day."

Cathy neglects answering. She pushes a handful of toilet articles into a corner of her suitcase, slams the lid and locks it.

"You're dusty all over with the rich glow of motherhood."

Philip stands up. "Look," he says, "we'll meet you at the boat." He is still showing concern.

Chris looks from the woman to the man and grins foolishly. Propping his bottle between the two pillows he launches himself to his feet with an impact that rattles the bedlamp.

"Sure," he says. He winks at Cathy and ducks out the door.

"What is it this time?" Cathy says.

"Farewell party. The *Berlin*."

"Farewell for who?"

"Nobody."

Cathy slips the blue cardigan over her shoulders and fastens one button at her throat. She is not wearing lipstick, but she compresses her lips as if she has just put some on.

"It's a farewell party for Phil Willing, the big poet," she says. "Goodbye, dreams."

Philip picks the bottle off the bed, dumps the rest of the beer down the sink and the bottle into the wastebasket. He rinses his hands and dries them on the threadbare towel by the sink. Cathy is waiting in the hall.

"Better hurry," she says.

He does hurry, apprehensive about repeating old arguments. His mouth is dry from anger—or desperation—suppressed in him.

"You're not wearing a coat," he tells Cathy.

"I know. I don't own one I can button."

She is first downstairs; when he has left the key at the desk she is already sitting in a taxi. He gets in beside her and instructs the driver.

"It's aimless," Cathy says.

He is resolved not to answer, but broods, smoking, as the cab rattles past monotonous gray apartment houses on the way to the docks. At the customs gate the car stops; an American soldier leans down to the window.

"We're seeing some friends off on the *Berlin*," Philip says.

The soldier touches his cap and passes them through. Ahead, at the end of a dirt road, is the cement bulk of the Columbus Bahnhof —where Philip and the others docked the day before. A passenger train is half-devoured by the building; a loading crane moves ponderously beyond and above it.

The car stops near the edge of the quai; Philip pays the driver and gets out. As he helps Cathy, she says:

"It's all right for Sal and Jenny. They aren't married."

She keeps his hand and squeezes it gently. Philip tolerates the pressure to lead her aboard the ship.

As they pause in a mirrored, marbled corridor outside the third-class lounge of the *Berlin*, Cathy turns toward him. She puts her hands to her belly.

"I can't go in there," she says. "They'll trample me."

Philip urges her into the room. "Don't be silly," he tells her. She lets herself move sullenly ahead of him.

The lounge is jammed. It is dark, gloomily paneled, lighted now by scores of faces, noisy with laughter and talk mostly in German. It is as if half of Germany is beginning a voyage to North America, and the other half has come to cheer. Three bartenders pour liquor and dispense beer. There is a continual movement toward the bar of men with heads low, shoulders hunched, empty glasses in their fists. Away from the bar moves an equal current of men, heads and shoulders stiffly back—sometimes with elbows close to their chests and the filled glasses riding at cheek level, sometimes with arms raised so the drinks barely clear the light fixtures. The center of the room is open for traffic; small tables and chairs are along the walls.

"This is a peach of a time for an abortion," Cathy says. She is trying to smile—to make up with him.

They push to one side of the lounge, skirting tables and chairs. No one moves out of their way, no one objects to their shoving. A face— Damon's, thin and rabbity—suddenly appears.

"Sweets!" he cries. He is looking at Philip, but kisses Cathy roughly on the forehead. "The girls are in the corner." He gestures over his shoulder and twists his body to let her past. Philip lets her go.

"Big party," he says.

"A brawl," Damon answers. "Come help with the liquor."

Philip follows Damon to the bar.

"What are you drinking? Scotch?"

"Sure," Philip says.

Damon buys six whiskies and passes three of them back to Philip. They begin the precarious trip to a table with the drinks held high over their heads.

"Cathy doesn't drink Scotch." Philip shouts this.

"These are for us," Damon calls back. He stops abruptly, pointing; Philip sees two vacant seats at a littered table. Damon lunges into one of the chairs, and Philip sits across from him, feeling whisky dribbling over his fingers. Damon clears the table simply, sweeping his arm across it; the fall of glass and debris is scarcely audible.

"You owe me a mark-fifty," Damon says. He arranges his three glasses in a line and appraises them. "You can pay me on the train."

"What comes after Rome?"

"I'm not certain. Take a drink," Damon orders.

Philip gulps his first whisky; it clears the lounge smoke from his throat and he feels awake for the first time today.

"I thought about Athens," Damon is saying. "It's a real thing now to lap up the Golden Age. And it's cheap."

"I don't know," Philip says vaguely.

"What don't you know?" Damon's green eyes study him with a special brightness—drunkenness, but with no loss of energy.

"All this flitting around."

"That what Cathy thinks?"

"Yes," Philip says. She is convenient for blame.

"Have a drink," Damon repeats.

"And me, too," Philip adds. He drinks the second Scotch and sets the empty glass inside the first. "I have to stop somewhere and do a little work."

"You think we don't know that?"

"No. No, I think *you* do." He begins to feel sheepish.

"We just got here," Damon says. He sips his liquor slowly, not taking his eyes off Philip. "Maybe you should go back to teaching, huh?"

"I don't miss that," Philip says. He thinks of Cathy. "All this drifting," he begins, but fails to finish.

Over the noise behind him he can hear the metallic accents of a loudspeaker. He does not know what is said, or what language it is said in, but he guesses it has to do with the sailing. There is a drift of people toward the exits. He looks to Damon, but Damon dismisses the unspoken idea of going ashore by a wave of his hand.

"Just tell me one thing," Damon says. "What does a poet want?" If he is drunk, he asks the question soberly.

"How should I know?" Philip answers. He is annoyed.

"What do *you* want?" Damon puts his hand on Philip's arm and holds on. "You write a lot of junk, Phil, but you write a little poetry. I don't care a damn about the junk."

Philip shrugs.

"A reputation?"

"I never write a single line with the least shadow of public thought." Philip spins out the borrowed words; a feint, a defense. Damon's grip is painful, and the hurt jumps to his brain, where it throbs and makes him dizzy. It is the whisky, and smoke, and being commanded to say the passionate word.

"What the devil do you want?" Damon repeats.

"Not the name," says Philip, "but the remembering of it." He wrenches the arm away and folds his hands under the table. Leaning forward, he says: "It scares me, Damon. It scares me I'll never get it."

Damon shakes his head, pitying. "Fame." He pronounces it with an odd laugh. "Poor old fame."

"Let's forget it," Philip says. Sorry to have forced the word, he stands up scowling and turns away. He catches sight of Cathy in a far corner of the room; she is at a table with Jenny and Sally and Chris—yet she is alone. The other three are arguing; Cathy sits apart, looking vaguely about her. When Philip succeeds in meeting her eyes, she shakes her head and glances away.

"You ought to be scared," Damon is saying. He drinks a whisky and drops the glass on the floor. "There's no immortality in the Twentieth Century—not even for the Immortals."

Philip nods and sits down, as if he agrees. In fact, he is uncertain. He remembers that Damon is going to reform the world—with art, with poetry, with a Golden Age—and he keeps silent. The lounge gradually empties; all the visitors have left the ship, and the travelers are lining the rails to weep and wave farewells. The six Americans and the two German bartenders are left.

"Let's get off," Philip says.

They band together. Cathy takes Philip's arm and clings harder than she needs to. Chris smirks. Sally and Jenny whisper together.

On deck they are confronted with an unbroken barrier of railing.

The covered gangplank is pulled away from the side of the ship.

"Canada, here we come," Damon says.

"Oh, God," Cathy murmurs.

Chris whirls on a white-jacketed officer nearby. "How do we get off?" He points at the shore. "Off this silly ship."

The officer understands. He beckons and they follow him aft—Damon and Jenny in the lead, Chris with Sally, Philip and Cathy last. They are led down a series of narrow metal companionways which the German officer negotiates at incredible speed.

"Don't go too fast," Cathy says on each ladder. "Don't pull me."

"I'm not," Philip says. "I'm not."

They find themselves deep in shadow, looking toward a rectangle of daylight. The officer points; Damon thanks him.

"It's the crew's gangway," Damon says.

"Like a railroad," says Jenny, "without the tracks."

"Be careful," Cathy says.

"*You* be careful," Philip replies.

He is behind her as they make their way down the narrow plank studded with crosspieces. Only a few paces from the end of it, Cathy stumbles. She catches at his sleeve, loses her grasp, and before he can reach out or shout for Chris to turn, she has gone sprawling onto the cobbled quai.

Later, Philip will not remember that she cries out—only that as she strikes the ground she twists her body violently to lie on her side, and that she draws her knees close to her. He kneels beside her and speaks her name.

Her eyes are open; her lower lip is white under her teeth. "Get a doctor," she says, breathless. "Please, Phil."

Philip looks up at the others.

Damon says: "Chris, better call an ambulance."

"Where should I call one?"

"At a hospital. Maybe there's an army hospital."

Chris jogs away.

"It'll be all right, sweetie," Sally says.

"Phil?" Cathy draws his hand to her face. "You won't leave me here?"

"Don't be silly." He can think of nothing gentle.

She forces a smile, her eyes still astonishingly open. "We should have gone to Canada," she says in a thin voice.

Chris is back in minutes. "You were right," he says. "The army's got a hospital, and I ordered an ambulance."

"Did they say how long?" Philip asks.

"Quick." Chris turns to Damon. "I also got us a cab."

"Do you need us?" Damon asks.

"No," says Philip. "No, go ahead."

Damon bends over the woman. "It's going to be okay, Cathy," he says. "Don't you worry."

"I'm all right," Cathy says. She puts her lips against her husband's hand.

Damon squeezes Philip's shoulder. "See you at the train; ten o'clock." He straightens up and leads the others away. Chris is saying: "I had a hell of a fight with that Kraut payphone. It was like a slot machine."

As he crouches alone beside his wife, Philip feels as if he is in an enormous arena. Behind him the *Berlin* is moving away from the dock, tugboats nudging at bow and stern. Before him the second-story railing of the *Bahnhof* is lined with bandsmen playing, and with people weeping, waving, cheering the departure. It is the cheering that particularly unsettles him, and makes him think the waiting is more tedious than it ought to be.

What finally does come for Cathy is a boxy, olive-drab sedan-truck with red crosses flamboyant on its panels. It skids to a stop beside Philip; two men in army fatigues and field jackets launch themselves out of the cab and run to him.

"What's up?" one of them asks.

"She fell," Philip says.

"Any bones broken?"

"I don't think so. She's going to have a baby."

The second soldier has opened the rear doors of the van and dragged out a stretcher. He puts it on the ground by Cathy.

"Don't you worry, Mrs.," he says. "We got very good doctors."

"Help me move her," the first soldier says. "You'll have to let go his hand, lady, just till we get you in the vehicle."

Philip feels his hand released, cool. Cathy puts her own hands against her mouth and closes her eyes.

"She don't want to go on her back," one of the men says.

"Put her on just like she is. Don't do anything clumsy."

They ease her onto the stretcher, still on her side. As they slide the stretcher into the van, she moans—the first animal sound Philip has heard her make.

"Give her something," the first soldier tells his partner inside the ambulance. He holds the doors open while Philip climbs in, then he shuts and latches them.

There is small light in the van; Philip fumbles his way to a narrow bench dropped down from a side wall and sits at one end of it. The soldier moves away from the woman, shoves a small bag under the bench, and settles himself at the other end. He raps at the tiny window into the cab, finds and lights a cigarette. The ambulance lurches.

Cathy does not ask for the return of Philip's hand, nor does he offer it. He sits uneasily while the truck bounces and rattles toward a hospital he hopes is close by.

"I gave her a little something," the soldier tells him. "Not a drug or anything—just a kind of tranquilizer."

Philip nods.

"She's preggy, huh?"

"Yes."

"How far along?"

"Eight months, about."

"Well," the soldier drawls, "she is sure going to have it."

Philip sits with his elbows on his knees, his hands folded, looking down at Cathy. She has taken one handle of the stretcher in both her hands and holds it hard.

"You army?" the soldier asks.

"No."

"Special Services?"

"No. Tourist."

"Hell of a way to see Germany," the soldier says. He grinds the cigarette under his heel and slumps into the corner.

Philip is looking at Cathy, but his thoughts are of the others. He does not blame them for leaving him at the dock: his family trials are none of their concern, and their particular uses of freedom are none of his. He feels guilty for what has happened. He wonders how much he will upset the planning which has brought them to Europe, and he wonders how this day of his life will affirm or destroy Damon's ambition for them all. On this impulse he reaches into his coat pocket and draws out his billfold. It is fat with the money he and Cathy have saved for the trip—most of it in traveler's checks, the rest in hundred-dollar bills. He counts out three of the bills and puts the money into the breast pocket of his shirt behind the pack of cigarettes.

The soldier has been watching. "You got any greenbacks?"

"What?" Philip says. He is sweating, for no reason he can imagine. His voice is hollow in the narrow van.

"U.S. currency. You got any with you?"

"A little."

"I can get you five marks on the dollar for greenbacks," the soldier says.

"No thanks."

"I can maybe get you five-twenty. That's better than you can do for yourself," the soldier says. "Same deal on traveler's checks—so long as they're not signed."

Philip shakes his head. The soldier sighs and smokes again.

Then the ambulance stops, backs, stops again. The doors open, flooding in light. Philip jumps to the ground; the two corpsmen jostle the stretcher out of the van.

"This way," the driver says.

The truck has come under a narrow arch and into a paved courtyard. The hospital, a half-dozen floors of red brick, surrounds the court on three sides. Philip follows at some distance as the two men carry his wife into one of several entrances. By the time he reaches the building, Cathy is nowhere to be seen, and he is in a high ceilinged lobby looking down an empty corridor.

"Sir?" A small, dark nurse stands up from a desk in one corner of the lobby.

"They just brought my wife in," he says, gesturing vaguely.

"Yes, sir. They've taken her up." She turns, motioning Philip to follow. "Would you sit here, please?"

She returns to the desk. He sits before her, watching as she goes through a ritual of opening drawers, taking out cards and papers, arranging them.

"Your full name?" she says, poising a fountain pen.

"Philip Willing."

"And your wife?"

"Catherine." He spells the name.

"Are you a civilian?"

"Yes." He fumbles after a cigarette and lights it. "We've just arrived here."

"Then you are not personnel assigned to this port?"

"No."

"I see." Everything she says disowns communication. "Your age?"

"Thirty-one."

"Your wife's?"

"Twenty-eight."

And so on. It is a tedious cross-examination, endless. By now the liquor he has drunk earlier is wearing off, and his lips and throat are dry. He is fidgeting, licking his lips and swallowing hard, when a tall figure approaches from the corridor. The nurse swings around in her chair.

"Doctor Magnus," she says, "this is the woman's husband."

Magnus stops beside the desk. He is a tall, incredibly straight man, slender but not thin, with severe features. His manner is military as he takes up the admission forms to read.

"I'm almost finished," the nurse says.

"Quite so," Magnus tells her, "but I will complete them in my office." He surveys Philip. "Mr. Willing?"

"Doctor." The word scratches his throat.

"Come with me, if you would be so kind."

Philip follows into a small room off the lobby. The office smells of

pipe tobacco. The furnishings are of leather and dark wood; casement windows overlook the courtyard.

"Please sit," Magnus says. "I have put your wife in the care of
Major Morris. He is American, excellent with mothers."

"Thank you," Philip says.

Magnus sits at his desk. "These forms," he says, sorting them on
the desk-top. Philip keeps quiet; the doctor looks at him, through
him. "You should have to wait not long," he says. "It will be a normal birth; more difficult, but normal."

"I'm glad to know that." The doctor's brittle attention and pre-
cise English unnerve him.

"A terrible experience," Magnus concludes. He takes a mechani-
cal pencil from the breast pocket of his coat and lays the point
against the papers. "Have you been long in Germany?"

"Since yesterday," Philip answers. He glances toward the windows, sees the flat gray color of a sky that is neither morning nor
evening, and becomes unexpectedly confused. "No, no," he stam-
mers, "the day before yesterday."

"Which?" says Doctor Magnus.

The doctor's eyes are yellow, like a cat's, with enormous pupils
that exploit every shred of light in the dim office. Looking into them,
Philip feels confusion mastering him. "Thursday," he says hoarsely.
It is the limit of his ability to commit himself.

"That is yesterday," says Magnus, making a note.

"Yes. Yesterday. Around noon."

Magnus writes. He is busy for a long time. Philip sits uneasily in
the leather chair, listening to sounds from the corridor of heels,
empty-place voices, the click and echo of doors; he wonders what the
doctor is doing to the simple fact of his arrival, yesterday, around
noon.

"Are there more questions?" Philip asks.

Magnus stops working and taps the pencil on the desk.

"Do you have to ask any more questions?" Philip repeats.

"There are a few," the doctor says, "for the sake of the records."
He makes more pencil marks. "You are American?"

"Yes."

"And your work? Your vocation?"

"Writer." After seven months, is it a lie?

"I see."

"And teacher," Philip adds. A hedge.

"Of course. And who should be notified, in the event of problems touching upon your wife's accident?"

Philip is startled by the question. Anger occurs to him; it is poised in his mind as he says: "*I* am her husband."

"*Natürlich*," says Magnus. An indulgent smile flickers on his features, and he taps the pencil once, twice, against the knuckles of his left hand. "We like also another name. Your wife's parents, perhaps. Some permanent address."

"I don't see why—"

"It is not so important, Mr. Willing."

Magnus secures the pencil in his pocket and pushes his chair away from the desk. When he stands, he tucks his hands into the pockets of the long coat and walks toward the windows. He seems interested in the dull sky.

"The Americans in Bremerhaven have a joke," he says irrelevantly, "that last year spring was a Friday afternoon."

Philip waits.

"I should like to ask you questions which have nothing to do with records," Magnus says. "Will you take offense?"

"No," says Philip, not knowing.

"In America, did your wife have a doctor to consult?"

"Yes."

"She is how many months pregnant?"

"About eight."

"And the doctor? He called your attention to the dangers of a long journey? Fatigue. Unusual movement. The possibility of risk in unfamiliar surroundings?"

"We didn't discuss our plans with the doctor."

Magnus sits, stiffly, on a corner of the desk. "But the steamship agents? They raised a question, did they not?"

"It was a fairly large ship," Philip says. "Adequate."

"And from here, where were you going?"

"A number of places. Switzerland. Italy."

"I presume by train."

"Yes."

"You are foolish," Magnus says. He leans over to open the top desk drawer and brushes the papers into it. "You are a foolish man, and an incomprehensibly lucky one."

Philip gets up, feeling shaky. "Is that all?" he asks.

Doctor Magnus shrugs. "If you wish," he replies. He is once more interested in the sky as Philip leaves the office.

In the lobby Philip stops at the reception desk. The nurse looks up expectantly.

"Do you have an envelope?" he asks her.

"Yes, certainly." She rummages until she finds one. Philip takes the three hundred dollars from his shirt and puts the money into the envelope; he seals it and writes *Catherine Willing* across the front of it. "Would you keep this for me?"

The nurse takes the envelope and reads the name.

"The fact is," Philip hastens to lie, "I didn't bother to buy traveler's checks when we left New York. I'm going out to get something to eat, and I don't want to lose this."

She smiles. "Of course, Mr. Willing. I'll have Doctor Magnus lock it up for you."

She goes directly to the office he has just left, before Philip can find the voice to call her back. He does not wait for her reappearance.

Outside the hospital arch he hails a cab and goes directly to the hotel. It is a trip of several miles; the fare takes the last of the few German coins he has, and by the time he gets his key and goes to his room a heavy bell nearby is tolling seven. He switches on the light and goes back to close the door; in the hall he finds the desk clerk, looking apologetic, holding out a folded paper.

"This," the clerk says. He seems to want to say more.

Philip takes the paper. "Thank you very much," he says, and closes the door gently. The note is in Damon's bad hand. It reads: *Next door—come drink.*

Philip crumples the paper into the wastebasket. He wants no

party. It is a novelty to be alone and free, and he tries—finding a stubby pencil on the floor beside the bed and the empty folder for the steamer tickets in his pocket—to write a poem about himself and his freedom. Failing—because he is out of practice, or because he has chosen a bad subject—he puts his materials aside and stretches out on top of the bed. He puts a cigarette to his lips, realizes he does not want to smoke, and falls asleep. He has no useful dreams.

He is awakened some time later by the furious pressure of hands at his shoulders. Chris, reeking of beer, hovers over him.

"Where you been?" Chris says.

"Here," Philip answers. His head throbs and his mouth tastes like sleep. "The hospital, then here."

"Damon wants you."

"I can't, Chris. I can't drink now."

"Who said drink?"

"That's what it always is."

"Maybe he wants to talk."

"No," Philip says, and he tries to lie down. Chris takes him under the arms and pulls him upright beside the bed.

"Look," he says, "are you with us?"

Philip is wholly awake; he picks up his coat, and follows Chris down the stairs and out of the hotel. Outside, Chris punches him playfully on the arm. "Relax," he says; he stops in front of a bar-room, opens the door and gestures Philip inside.

It is a small room, poorly lighted, with a short, mirrored bar against the far wall, and under the windows to the left a long, shallow aquarium boiling with green water and tiny fish darting in and out of algae and coral castles. A fat bartender, enormously jowled and red in the face, waves to Philip. Damon and the two girls are at a round table close by the bar; he seems to be playing solitaire while Jenny and Sally look on.

Chris pushes Philip forward. "See what I found."

Damon glances up from his cards. "Philip Willing," he says. "Philip Willing come liquor-swilling."

"I fell asleep," Philip says.

"Likely," Damon answers. He kicks a chair out from the table;

Philip sits down. Damon shuffles the cards and begins dealing them face up around the table. "Jacks," he says.

The deal continues. The first knave turns up in front of Chris. "Triple cognac," he says. He signs to the bartender.

The second jack comes to Jenny. She takes the drink from the counter and touches it briefly to her lips.

The third jack falls to Philip. He protests: "I don't want to start drinking again."

Philip drains the glass. The brandy is hot, welcome. He coughs self-consciously and puts the glass on the table.

Chris accepts the fourth jack, and pays. The deal passes.

For two hours the game goes on, and during it nothing is said about Cathy, or about a train to Basel, or about a choice between them. Damon does not tease Philip about fame, or chide him over responsibilities, or preach to him about art. Only much later does it occur to Philip that the third jack is usually his, and that most of the drinks are multiple shots of cognac. Once he excuses himself to go to the men's room, and there he leans dizzily over the urinal, his hands against the discolored wall tiles supporting him while he vomits and tries to remember where he is. When he comes out, ready in an automatic, mindless way to resume the drinking game, Damon and Chris are in wait outside the door.

"Train time," Chris says.

"Listen," Philip says. "No, no." When he pulls free he loses his balance and starts to fall.

"The road to Athens," Damon says, catching him.

Of the chaos to follow, Philip will remember a blurred glimpse of the bartender's chins trembling over cognac glasses, and the shimmering street, and his face cool under a light rain. There is a taxi—small and absurdly uncomfortable. He rides in the rear seat, his head against a window, his feet hung over the front seat between Damon and the driver. When the cab reaches the railroad station he is dragged feet-first out of the car. He waits, unsteady, his mind sluggishly pursuing the idea that he is keeping an appointment. Damon is beside him, taking his arm, magically holding his briefcase out to him.

"Here's your work," Damon says.

Philip takes it; it seems weightless. He stumbles along beside Damon, who opens a door for him. They pass through a noisy, musty waiting room where people and benches are fuzzy under a haze of smoke. On the platform the air is cleaner and cooler, and the confusion behind him is diminished to a whisper high up in the curved darkness. The train is ahead of them.

Their tickets are for a third-class carriage, a spare, wooden interior lit violently by bare bulbs. The benches are occupied by plump old women in kerchiefs, gray men in seamen's caps, children with uncovered, stunning blond hair. Philip sits by the aisle and pushes his briefcase under the seat. Now he is aware of reflections in the window glass, and of objects moving beyond the reflections. He feels his hand touched.

"It'll be fine, Phil," he hears Jenny say.

The train lurches ahead. Feeling the movement, gradually comprehending it, he forces himself to stand.

"I'm sick," he says. He wonders if he really is.

He ropes gracelessly up the aisle and stops between cars. It is noisy, and he tastes a slowly growing draught of air; the side door has not yet been shut; the gray station pavements slip past. Philip plunges forward, down three narrow steps, and for an instant hangs poised in the opening. He guesses that the train has passed out of the station, and then he lets go. As he comes to the ground, limp and tumbling, he thinks he hears his name.

"WILLING!"

The voice might be Damon's—it sounds much like it, a strong shout over the noise of the train. But life is all loud; he thinks this as he falls, feeling his senses smothered by the train, by the word that might be his own name, by the dull throb of drink against his skull. It is difficult to separate things; he cannot decide which is the murmur of continuous movement, which the whispered suggestion of fame, which the pulse of alcohol. Rolling down the wet embankment, feeling grass and gravel coarse against his hands and face, he looks up to see the train lurching past, creaking and piping loud. Its lighted windows one by one blur before his eyes. In the windows are the faces of the others, distinct but scarcely aware of him; as the last lights vanish he stops falling and passes out in the dark and the silence of drenched earth.

When next he opens his eyes Philip is lying on a padded leather table. The surroundings seem familiar—a small room furnished with a desk of dark wood, a walnut coat rack, a low table with a metal sterilizer glistening on it. He smells pipe tobacco. Raising himself on one elbow he sees light outside the narrow casement windows; dawn or dusk—he does not know which.

His head aches. His neck muscles are stiff and his whole body feels vaguely as if he has lain a long time on a bare floor. He discovers that his suit is streaked with dirt; a three-corner tear is open at the knee of one trouser leg. When he tries to remember, the events of his boarding and leaving the train seem improbable.

A door opens. He sits up slowly. "Doctor Magnus," he says.

"I'm delighted you are awake," Magnus says. "We were disturbed."

"I guess I had myself a night," Philip says. He is embarrassed. "I had this peculiar . . . accident." Magnus extends a pack of American cigarettes. Reaching out to take one, Philip notices that his hand is bandaged. "How did I get this?"

"Your peculiar accident. A small thing."

"Stupid," Philip says. He talks around the cigarette. "I left something on a train. Do you suppose I'll get it back?"

"Money?"

Philip puts his hand to the inside pocket of his jacket; he is relieved to feel the billfold.

"No," he says. "Not money."

Magnus pretends a smile. "It is hard to know what will happen with trains."

"I know." It occurs to him that Damon will have the briefcase—that he will likely not mail it back.

"One can only tell the authorities," Magnus says.

Philip is annoyed. Since entering the room, Magnus has stood in one place, watching, studying. If the doctor intends a medical pronouncement, why doesn't he get to it? Except for the nagging of his bruised muscles, Philip feels well. He feels, surprisingly, better than he has for some months. Still, good health aside, Philip is irritated by the German. He wonders if Magnus knows what is in the envelope locked in this room.

"I am most pleased to find you recovered," Magnus repeats, "to remind you of your wife. She is in the delivery room."

Something—fatigue, or drink, or design—has made Philip forget about the baby.

Magnus turns his back. "Major Morris is with her."

"May I talk with her?"

"Later, after the child is delivered." Doctor Magnus pauses at the door. "If you wish," he ends formally.

"Certainly I wish." Philip is trembling, partly from anger, partly from the curious guilt this man forces upon him.

"It is the third floor. There are chairs."

Philip slides down from the table; his left knee hurts and he stands unevenly. "Please show me," he says.

Taller than Philip, the doctor responds from what seems a level of divine condescension. "Of course, Mr. Willing."

Limping slightly, Philip follows him along the corridor into a roomy stairwell. The light is harsh yellow after the dimness of the office. Soft-drink and candy machines stand along one wall; a German janitor is swinging a damp mop over the tiled floor. At the bottom of the stairs Philip steps over a sallow young man in army fatigues reading a tabloid. The man glances up; his expression conveys contempt for the doctor, indifference to Philip.

At the second landing, out of breath and frowning from the ache in his knee, he follows Magnus down the disinfected hall to the door of the delivery room. Three chairs stand in a neat row along the wall. Magnus motions Philip into one of them.

"You will wait here," he says.

Philip sits down, gladly, his legs weak from climbing. Magnus raps at the door, goes inside, and reappears at once.

"Soon," he says, and goes away.

Philip folds his arms. Alone, without cigarettes, he finds the waiting tedious. There is nothing in the corridor to look at; nothing to do with his hands; nothing but the boredom of sitting still. He listens for Cathy—for a groan, a cry, some message of pain from behind the closed door. He hears nothing, only interior, early-morning silence.

In this perfection of inactivity it is easy for him to read meaning into the actions of the others—to know that Magnus's coldness measures his irresponsibility, that Damon's impatience deplores his weakness as artist, that Catherine's distress cries her domesticity and his failure to minister to it. He is astonished that in his own half-intentioned actions he finds no meaning at all. It is true, what he has told Cathy, that he does not know what to expect. He has never known. Life is not susceptible to him; it holds back answers. Even his poetry is an evasion, a synthetic stronger than fact but more fragile than philosophy, an escapist rewording of the hard problems.

He is roused from waiting by a woman's voice saying his name. A nurse—old, capless, in a soiled white uniform—is beckoning to him. By the time he reaches the delivery room she has gone inside, then emerges, pushing ahead of her a cart that bears his wife and his new child. Nothing in this new vision of Cathy is calculated to please him; she lies with one hand awkwardly palm-up over her belly, the other half-clasping the baby; her head lolls to one side, her eyes are swollen; small white accretions of salt cling to her cheeks; a line of dried blood rims the inside of her lower lip, and flakes of blood show on her teeth; the dark hair at her brow is matted from sweat.

Beside her, its head cradled against her throat, the baby lies like some pathetic, found animal, a creature of incredibly tiny features and fists. Without hair, eyebrows, lashes, its skin vaguely yellow save for tinges of pink throbbing at its temples and smears of thick blood on its shoulders and head, it looks like soft clay twisted into a clumsy imitation of childness and put aside to be fired. Both mother and baby are swaddled in layers of dingy gray linens.

Cathy puts out her hand to him.

"Say hello to your new daughter," she whispers.

"Is everything all right?"

"Yes," Cathy says. "Oh, yes."

An odd thought comes to Philip. "I envy you," he says.

"I kept telling them it had to be a boy. The doctor said you wouldn't mind."

"I don't."

"Did the doctor tell you that?"

"I haven't seen him."

"He said you wouldn't mind." She turns her head so her cheek touches the baby's forehead. "You really don't mind?"

"No."

"She's perfect, Phil. I counted her fingers and toes—that was the first thing I did. I was scared that she wouldn't be perfect, but she is. She's beautiful, isn't she?"

He kisses Cathy on the forehead, as if answering.

"I saw everything," she murmurs. "I was never out. They kept telling me to push harder and the doctor said, 'Come on, you can do better than that,' and all at once he held her up for me to see. He laid her across my stomach while they sewed me up, and then they took her away to wash some of the blood off. More than six pounds, the doctor thought." She presses Philip's hand. "God, Phil, I'm so tired."

The old nurse comes back into the hall. "I must take the baby now," she says.

"They'll come get me, too, in a minute," Cathy says. "Will you be all right in that hotel room by yourself?"

"Why not?"

"Wasn't it marvelous she could be born in an American hospital? Even the doctor was American."

"We were lucky," Philip says. He looks down at Cathy's pale face slack with fatigue; he tries to think of something affectionate to say. "The others are on the way to Italy," he reports finally. "I saw them off last night."

"I'll miss them. I thought you might leave me here and go with them."

"I didn't."

"Forgive me, Phil, for even imagining a thing like that."

He kisses her once more, then takes his hand from hers. "You'd better get some rest," he says. He knocks at the door of the delivery room; it opens and a second nurse looks out. "You can take her back in now," Philip tells the nurse.

"Come this afternoon," Cathy says. "We have to pick out a perfect name. And bring my little overnight case."

By way of answer he puts his fingers to his lips, signifying fondness across the growing distance between them as his wife is taken away.

He limps to the end of the hall, looking out a window pushed open on the damp morning. Over the rooftops of Bremerhaven he sees the long sheds and the angular loading cranes of the docks, far off against a dim horizon he imagines to be the North Sea. The wet spring wind carries in to him the reed voice of a train whistle; it reminds him of the lost manuscripts and of his own name ringing in his ears as he rolled over and over into the gully alongside the tracks. Below him, in a street shiny with cobblestones, a young man rides past on a bicycle, bobbing his head in time to a music Philip cannot hear. Watching the single rider glide out of sight, he feels a sense of loss that is entire—and not to be defined by any familiar word.

Visions

"I don't mean to give you the idea the place is haunted," Duncan Law said as he felt through his pockets for matches. "I don't think we have ancestral ghosts that need exorcising, or familiars in the back bedrooms, or anything like that. But he did give me quite a start."

"I can imagine," Philip said.

The two men were standing in front of the house, on a grassy shelf that fell sharply away at their feet and sloped through granite outcroppings and scrub pines down to the ocean, several hundred yards distant. It was early morning; a heavy Maine fog still curled among the branches of the taller pines nearby and hung in layers over the descent to the sea. The house itself was in relief against a drab gray curtain, its white clapboards only beginning to show the pale reflection of a sun.

"He was right there, alongside that middle chimney." Law pointed with his right hand and opened a matchbook with his left. "When I got my first glimpse of him, he was balanced on the ridgepole, squatting, with his hands folded between his knees. He was laughing, but I couldn't hear anything—just saw his mouth open and his shoulders jogging. I must have turned away for a second or two; when I looked up again there was nothing to see."

He struck a paper match and held it to his cigarette. The match hissed, smoked mightily, but died without taking fire. Law dropped it and struck another which behaved like the first. Philip offered his lighter.

"Seasons of mists," Law said, inhaling the flame. "Nothing dries out until afternoon. War on mildew."

"How about the winters?"

"Last winter was our first one here," Law said. "Damp to the marrow; cold as hell." He glanced back up at the chimney. "That's some trick, teetering on the ridgepole. I'd been up there just the day before, mortaring some loose bricks. A man might as easily stand on an axe-blade as on the point of that roof."

"It looks in good shape." Philip tried to make the words seem not a change of subject. His host was a long time quiet, examining a stray thread of tobacco in the unlighted end of the cigarette. It was as if the remark were too real to be taken carelessly.

"It doesn't leak, if that's what you mean."

"More or less," Philip said.

"The shingles are pretty old—a few of them are missing here and there, blown off—but the house is older. The point is, the roofing has been replaced three or four times since the house was built."

"When was that?"

Law raised his eyes to the roof. "The year I was born." Philip waited. "It's sixty-one years old," Law said.

"In good shape," Philip said lamely. He had conceived the foolish idea that Law was trying to sell him the house.

"It is." Law had gone back to worrying the tip of the cigarette. With each strand of tobacco he picked out and dropped, a new frayed end appeared. The whole thing seemed to be falling apart in his hands.

"At first I thought it must have been some kid from around here, climbing on a dare." His voice sounded remote, much divorced from his physical concentration on tobacco threads. "But the more I thought about it, the more I remembered it wasn't a young face. He was little, all right, but he had the face of an adult."

"Any kids living in the neighborhood?" An awkward sort of question—but the problem was not one Philip could have anticipated during a visit to the home of his former teacher. And where did it say that a guest was obligated to share in the hallucinations of his host?

Law had all but destroyed the cigarette—had given up smoking it

—and stood committed to the task of removing the blunt, burning end from its slender cylinder by rotating the paper between his thumb and index finger.

"The Kennett boys," he said, "but they're just youngsters. We buy clams from them—sometimes—and the last two or three years they've helped me put the boat in; scraping and caulking, that sort of thing."

"Where do they live?"

"Just south." Law turned his back on the house and pointed off into the eddies of fog. "About a half-mile and closer to the shore. You can see their place when it's cleared off."

Philip moved behind and closer to Law, as if better to follow the gesture. When Law turned back, eyes already lifting toward his obsessive chimney, his gaze met Philip's squarely. A fleeting, embarrassed smile touched Law's mouth, and he looked down at his hands. The cigarette tip spun smoldering into the grass; he rolled the paper into a ball and let go of it.

"Perhaps we should go inside," he said.

Philip followed him, somewhat at a distance. He had not seen Law in nearly four years; he had remembered him as a teacher and writer of inflated self-regard—of posturings appropriate to his reputation at the Institute. Now the extravagances were draining away. Not age was taking them; Law looked the same, still youthful for his years, still wearing sport shirts open-collared for—today—a yellow silk scarf. He wore the familiar clean khakis and the leather sandals that had inspired self-conscious imitation among his protégés. The faintest traces of gray touched his nearly blond hair. But something, something a mind's reach beyond Philip, was happening.

Whatever it was had begun to happen within a half-hour of Philip's arrival the night before. The car unpacked, his daughter, Deborah, transferred whimperingly into bed, his own and Cathy's room found and claimed, Philip and Law had sat in the kitchen with a bottle between them. Philip had done most of the talking—talk that was inconsequential and reflected his fatigue from a day's driving. He did not now remember that he had said anything of the slightest interest, yet Law was entirely attentive to him. At one unsettling moment, when there was a bare silence to be filled, Law had put out his whisky glass across the table and touched it to Philip's—somberly, earnestly. The gesture was stunning; Law was no longer the man at whose home Philip drank beer while Law sipped from a snifter of brandy that danced to the lordly rotation of his wrist. He seemed not to be the literary prince whose power was the making or breaking of young writers. Four years earlier, when Law had helped him win a grant to travel in Europe, he knew that what his teacher had done for him was less a favor than an exercise in reputation—as if Law had said to him: "You wish time to write? I shall permit it."

Now, the night before, Philip had lain awake in the dark, contending with the *something* happening to Law; until he fell asleep he tried to read the destination of the man's slow, restless footsteps in the room overhead, while Cathy clung nervously to his arms, whispering: "Listen to him. Listen!" He listened, and he was ignorant and uneasy. Today the figure on the ridgepole had come to disturb him further.

"Here's good old Robinson," Law said loudly. The St. Bernard, tethered on a twenty-foot chain to a metal stake, danced clumsily at the sound of his name. Law stopped and pummeled the dog's back, waiting for Philip to catch up. "He's reached his growth since you saw him last," he said. He stroked the animal's huge head and went on toward the back door. Philip detoured around the limit of Robinson's chain. "We've had some good fun together, Robbie and I. Romping, sniping at squirrels."

"I'll bet," Philip said. *That* was stupid; he wanted to say that he remembered the dog unkindly, that Robinson—scarcely more than a puppy—had once knocked him flat on his back.

"About a year ago, some of the chaps in my seminar got together to gamble over Robbie. Wanted to have a pool on whether he was named after Jeffers or Edwin Arlington—"

"Or Swiss Family?"

Had Law heard him? "I told them I damned well didn't know if I'd named him after anybody, and they ought to know better than ask a poet where inspirations come from."

Philip nodded; this seemed a flash of the old Law—pompous and condescending, believing what his classes over and over heard him say: "My name is Law; my word is Law."

Framed by the open doorway, Law swept his arm in the direction of the ocean. "There," he said, "you can just make out the lines of an island. See it? They call that the Needle—it's a long, skinny ledge about a hundred yards out. The channel between here and the island is the Thread of Life. Clever? There'll be a good bit of boat traffic through there when the fog lifts." He squinted against the brightening sun. "Then way out—but you can't see it yet—is Monhegan. At night you can watch its lights."

Philip looked.

"Well, then," Law said, oppressively jovial, "the ladies must have the breakfast dishes done, so perhaps it's safe to go in."

He led Philip through the low shed that adjoined the kitchen. In the hall outside the kitchen door he slapped the top of an old wooden icebox. "We retired this just last year," he said.

When they entered, Cathy was at the kitchen table, mending a tiny white sock in front of a cup of coffee.

"Here's your wife," Law said. "Now where's Vivian?"

Cathy said: "She and Debbie went out to the road to see if the mail's here."

Law fished one of his pipes out of a canister in the center of the table and sat down with it opposite Cathy. Philip lounged, standing, against the sink.

"This is an awfully nice old house," Cathy said.

Law rocked back against the wall. "We bought it five years ago, as a summer retreat," he said. "The first summer I dug a new cesspool —all by myself, and it damned near finished me off—the second we put in electricity and got a telephone. Last year we bought a new refrigerator and stove, winterized the place, installed an oil burner. Now it's a retirement home."

"If you ever retire," Philip said.

Law was suddenly annoyed. "I'm not immortal," he said. "You don't have to play up to me." He let the chair come down hard on all its legs, and fumbled at the dead pipe.

Philip shifted his feet and could not think if he needed to make an apology. Cathy cast a sidewise look at him, but kept still. Law solved the awkwardness by leaving the kitchen.

"I better let Robinson in," he said. "There's no water out there."

"He isn't what I expected a famous poet to be like," Cathy said.

"He isn't what I expected, either," Philip said.

"He acts like one of the ghosts of Christmas."

"I'd like to know what's the matter with him."

"Is he a good poet?"

Philip shrugged. "As poets go," he said. He watched the St. Bernard precede its master into the room, take one lumbering turn around Cathy's chair, and collapse noisily to the floor between the stove and the sink.

"Moves like a silly bear," Law said, resuming his seat.

Philip waited. *As poets go* lingered in the room, just now reaching his own innermost ear in a voice like someone else's.

"Well, perhaps we should talk," Law said heavily.

"Should I go somewhere else?" Cathy asked.

"No, no." Law rubbed the pipestem along his nose. "The point is that it's mainly a question-and-answer business now."

Philip braced his palms against the edge of the sink. "Go ahead," he said. He wondered if any of the questions would be answers.

"You're still publishing?"

"Some poems in the quarterlies. I've got a book ready."

"I could talk to some people," Law said.

"It's not so important." He wondered how influential Law might be.

"Still pecking away at the novel?"

"Not enough; not since Europe."

"You never did tell me about Europe."

"You know," Philip said. "Deborah was born there. We came home early." He looked at Cathy; her eyes were down, as if reading from the sock in her hands the frictions of Europe.

"You like teaching?"

"Yes, pretty much."

Law rocked back in the chair. "I was thinking of recommending you to the Institute staff for next year."

"Are you serious?" Philip said. He thought: *Revelation.*

"We'll talk about it. I'm going away for a while."

"Some government thing?" Philip asked. Law seemed always off on "some government thing." Six years earlier, while Philip was still in school, it had been a literary mission to India. Only two years ago Law had gone to Africa, but he had come back to the States unexpectedly early.

Law grimaced. "You might say: Some sort of government thing."

"I'd very much like to talk about it," Philip said. He might have said more—trying not to seem tongue-tied from gratitude—but his daughter, and behind her Law's wife, came in from the front of the house.

Law stood up to take the mail. "Anything?" he said.

"Circulars," said his wife. She was small and slender, and but for her white hair she might have been no older than forty.

Deborah said: "Mommy, they have flowers growing right in the middle of the road!" She spoke this shrilly, then ran to Robinson and began patting him stiffly on the head. The kitchen seemed overcrowded and deafening; Philip made a move to draw his daughter away from the dog.

"That's all right," Law said. "He doesn't bite little girls."

"He's just a big, gentle baby, Philip," Vivian said.

Deborah quit petting the dog and placed herself in front of Law. "You're awfully tall, aren't you?" she said.

"I guess I am."

"That means you're very old. Are you a hundred?"

"Dibs!" Philip said.

Law shook his head. "How old are *you?*"

"I'm this much and a half," holding up three fingers.

"She was born in March," Cathy said.

"Debbie," Vivian said, "do you like blueberries?"

"I think so." Debbie frowned.

"I believe I know where there are a whole lot of blueberries in a big meadow not far from here. Let's you and me and Mommy go pick some for a pie."

"All right," Deborah said. She took Vivian's hand; to Law she said: "Do you know what I'm going to do?"

"What might that be?"

"I'm going to cut open your tummy and take out all your birthdays!"

Giggling, she went out the back door with Vivian; Robinson jerked to his feet and floundered after them. Cathy put down her sock, cast a helpless look at Philip, and followed.

Law sorted through the papers in his hand, then dropped them into a wastebasket under the sink drainboard. "I was thinking," he said almost irrelevantly, "that if you took the appointment you might like to live here. I'd throw that in, but you'd have to keep the place up."

"I'd like to talk about that, too. Cathy might enjoy it."

"Ninety-five hundred is all they'll pay you for two courses, but I imagine that's more than you'll get if you stay where you are now."

"Yes," Philip said.

Law stood at the window, looking out after the women. "It would have been nice to have a child," he said. "We never managed one, and I've thought I must have missed a good part of life—" Unexpectedly, he launched himself across the kitchen to the door. "Oh, God damn it," he muttered.

Philip went after him, startled, wondering what new vision the man had seen. Through the opened door he heard Robinson barking frantically, the women shouting, Deborah screaming, Law calling the dog's name. By the time Philip was outside, Law was already coming back, holding something in his hands.

"It's some dumb cat," Law said. "Cats are something Robbie *will* take a bite of."

"I think it belongs to the Kennetts," Vivian said behind him. "I'll call the vet."

"You might call the Kennetts, too," Law said, "and find me some kind of box."

"I'll look for one," Cathy offered. "It's my fault. I let him out." She turned to Philip, white-faced, the tears vivid in her eyes.

In the foolish shock of the moment, Cathy could not find dustrags or old sheeting, and she lined a shoebox with a pink doll's blanket belonging to Deborah. By the time the box was ready, the cat had died. It was small and gray with tiger stripes, hardly more than a kitten, and Law laid it grotesquely in the bottom of the box. Its matted fur still glistened with blood in so many places—its head and throat, its back and belly and paws—that there was no way for the eye to decide precisely where had been the real wounds and where were shining reflections of the real wounds.

Clearly, its body had been broken. From the look of the animal, Philip thought that either the neck, or the back, or both, had been snapped by the lash of the dog's attack. The kitten's head was skewed at a curious angle from the rest of the body; its delicate, triangular face was lopsided, as if the head had been crushed, and a glaze of blood coated the muzzle. Inside the ridges of the left ear a pool of blood was blackening.

Philip looked away. Law shrugged—a movement seeming more weary than indifferent.

"I don't think the Kennetts would like to see this," he said to Vivian. "Did you call them?"

"There wasn't any answer. I'll try again."

"No; I'll go over later and see if I can't explain."

"If you've got some kind of shovel," Philip said, "I could bury it in the woods."

Law shook his head. "No, this is my death to clean up. You can come along if you want."

"I will," Philip said.

"I'll get a shovel out of the barn," Law said. As he left the kitchen, Robinson trailed him. "Come along, Robbie."

Philip followed, pausing in the doorway to kiss Cathy on the forehead. "See if you can soothe Deborah," he said. "Make it into an adventure."

Cathy hugged her elbows. "I'll do my best; she's upstairs, crying."

Philip cradled the shoebox in one arm and went down the flagged path leading to the barn. Robinson pranced at the opened barn door; in a moment Law emerged. He had put on a denim jacket over his sportshirt and was carrying a long-handled shovel. Tucked into the waistband of his khakis was the barrel of a pistol—its grip squared and black.

"Where did that come from?" Philip said.

Law touched the weapon, gently, as if petting it. "I bought it, right after the war. Don't ask me why. I'd just gotten out of the army—I'd spent the better part of four years in England and France, playing policeman, wearing whistles and armbands and a white hat . . . and a pistol like this one. I guess I missed it, whatever it meant to me when I was so young. It was cheap; pawn shops were full of them." He raised the shovel so its handle rested on his left shoulder. "For a long time I forgot I owned it; then when we began moving ourselves up here, lo and behold it turned up—about a year ago. I'd gotten used to wearing a gun in Africa. I needed it there."

"Why carry it now?"

Law shook his head. "I don't have a sensible answer to a question like that. Now. Now I suppose I think of it as a kind of link with those old times—but that's an odd thing. I was so determined to use language, to use poetry as a way of helping to atone for all the bad actions of the war—I was going to be a true pacifist, a true apostle of peace—yet all the time I owned this piece, this barbarity. A chink in the armor."

"What was the reason for carrying a gun in Africa?"

"Oh," Law said, "that was *need*. The things one sees, the things one hears—" He looked narrowly at Philip. "It wasn't from the fear of racial murder, if that's what you think."

"No," Philip said. "No, of course not."

The two men had fallen into step toward the blueberry meadow, the dog circling them, crashing into the brush and leaves alongside the path.

"He's still excited," Law said. "I've never understood whether it's the killing, or only the exercise. I once asked a biologist friend of mine if adrenaline in animals is triggered the way it is in us. He didn't know; he wasn't even sure if animals were capable of excitement." Law shifted the shovel to his other shoulder. "He may have had the same ignorance about the human animal; he certainly was a cold fish himself."

"At least you can't blame a dog for killing a cat."

"I suppose it depends on how much you believe in the idea of domestication," Law said. "It ought to mean more than mere house-breaking."

"I don't think you can condition whatever it is that makes a hunter hunt."

Law chuckled. "That's a nice thought, of predation being above and beyond the rules. Godly." He stopped near a line of spruce that ran along the back edge of the meadow. "Here," he said. "This will do us." He took the pistol out of his belt, checked the safety catch, and slipped it into the pocket of his jacket; he buttoned the pocket flap.

Philip set the shoebox at the base of one of the scrub trees. "Let me do the honors," he said.

"No, no," Law said, "I'm capable." He put the point of the shovel against the earth and drove the blade in with a blow of his heel. Against the leverage of the handle the roots of dry grass broke with a sound like cloth tearing. "How deep do you think?" Law said.

"A foot or two?"

"I expect so." He gasped as he turned the dirt aside. "Still, I'll make it a little more generous. Something—there's always something—will come around, find this fresh dirt, dig into it. Fox. Rac-coon. Somebody else's dog."

"More likely Robbie himself," Philip said.

"No. I don't think Robbie." Law smiled a wry smile. "Which is the more offensive," he asked Philip: "the notion of being the one dug up, or the one digging? Corpse or ghoul?"

"Christ," Philip said, "don't make me think about it." *Or about poor Robinson.* He watched his host dig.

"Right," Law said at last. "That should be deep enough. Let's have the innocent."

Philip retrieved the shoebox. Robinson circled him, pushing at the box with his muzzle. "Easy, boy," Philip said. He raised the box above his head.

The hole was indeed generous. When Philip knelt and laid the shoebox into the grave, the box seemed tinier than even the dead kitten required.

"You did a lot of extra work," Philip said.

"All my life," Law said. He had sat down, cross-legged, not far from the mound of earth he had dug out, and he had managed to light a cigarette with one of his own damp matches.

"Shall I do the filling in?"

"I think the Kennett children might like a moment of quiet respect. No fancy business."

"As you say."

"You can head back to the house, if you'd like. I have to say my goodbyes to Robbie."

Philip saw that the pistol now lay in the angle of Law's crossed ankles. *How should I talk to this old man?* he thought. "You can't really mean to shoot Robbie."

Law ground out his cigarette in the dirt pile beside him. He held the pistol in both hands. "I've never had as much control over my life as I wanted," he said. "I think Vivian expected more of me."

"I don't know what you're saying."

"I'm saying I don't appreciate being judged by you, any more than I like being catered to." Law stood. "Here, Robbie," he said.

Philip turned away and started across the field toward the house, its shingled roof nearly obscured by birches and tall pines. He could see the central chimney and much of the ridgepole; no one was crouched there, no one laughing. When he came out of the small woods that contained the meadow, he was still several hundred feet from the house. The last shreds of fog had receded over the water below him; a thin mist hung in the pines that grew on the Needle.

Finally he heard the single shot fired. He stopped and waited, kneeling in the high grass, finding and eating a few blueberries from a stunted bush close at hand, until he heard Law approaching him.

"I always wanted to be famous," Law said. "I always wanted to hear my name spoken by others." He held the shovel before him, poking its tapered blade at roots across the path, letting the blade bounce ahead as he walked. The pistol was pushed inside the belt of his khakis.

Philip stayed silent. Perhaps he's gone crazy, he thought. *Poor*

Robbie, he thought.

"I know you don't approve," Law said. "I don't give a damn about that. And I could give you all sorts of excuses: I'm going to be away; if I gave him to someone at the Institute, they'd have no place to run him; it's hard to afford a dog that big; and he's gotten unpredictable. I'm too old to carry the responsibility for what an animal that size might do to a child."

"It's none of my business," Philip said.

"I don't care what you think of all this," Law said. "But you understand, don't you?"

"Understand what?"

"*Don't* you?" Law insisted.

"I'm not sure," Philip said.

Law rested the shovel handle against the side of the shed and went in; he set the pistol on a high shelf above the unused icebox. As the two men entered the kitchen, Cathy looked up from the table where she and Vivian were drinking coffee.

"Debbie's all right," she announced. "I persuaded her the kitten had gone to a happier place."

"Probably true," Law said. He winked at his wife.

"Where's poor Robbie?" Vivian asked.

Philip looked at Cathy, trying to say with his eyes: *You won't believe this. Not ever.*

"I don't know," Law said. "Off exploring somewhere."

At a quarter to midnight Cathy took Deborah to the toilet, steering the half-awake child through her parents' bedroom and across the shabby kitchen linoleum to the bathroom, holding her precariously upright on the throne, leading her back to sleep. As she passed the big bed where Philip lay—he was still dressed but for his shoes, both pillows propped behind his head—Deborah stopped.

"Kiss Daddy," she said irritably, casting off Cathy with a twist of one shoulder.

"Please, Deb," Cathy said.

Philip rolled to the edge of the bed. "Here, Dibs," he said.

His daughter kissed him on the cheek, her eyes mostly closed.

" 'Night, Daddy," she murmured.

" 'Night, Dibs."

The girl went to bed. Philip lay back against his pillows, smoking a cigarette. He watched the smoke rise straight up for a couple of feet, then break sharply into snarls of pale blue thread.

Cathy came out of Deborah's room, closing the door. "It's a nice room," she said. "There's even a picture of Jack and the Beanstalk on the wall."

"It's not a bad old house," Philip said. He surveyed the room; it was commodious, low-ceilinged, with fading green paper on the walls; the frames of the two windows were enameled white, and there were dark green shades but no curtains. The room had an abundance of doors: one to the kitchen, another to the living room, a third opening into the parlor. A narrow bookcase—partly filled with ragged paperbacks—stood between the door to Deborah's room and a deep closet.

"Would you like to live here?"

He shrugged. "It has a lot of ways to get in and out."

"How many rooms do you suppose are upstairs?" Cathy stood half-in, half-out of the closet, undressing, slipping a blue nightgown over her head.

"Two? No, I guess three. There's the bedroom and his study, and there must be a second bedroom. But no upstairs bath."

"There's an old privy out back."

"One hole or two?"

"Oh, really, Phil."

She sat on the edge of the bed and passed him an ashtray from the one nightstand that held a lamp. He put out the cigarette and reached back over his head to grip the high brass railing of the bed with both hands.

"My grandmother's house was like this," he said. "This brass bedstead could have been hers. And those floorboards—a foot wide. She had a dining room floor like that, my grandmother."

"I hope you noticed they have one of those precious iceboxes you're always raving about," Cathy said.

"But they don't use it."

"Well, at least they *have* it."

"It's not the same." He got up and undressed.

Cathy watched him. "If you're not going to wear your pajamas," she said, "look out."

Naked, he pulled back the covers of the bed and crawled in under them. "Look at this," he said. "Patchwork quilts a mile deep."

"A good thing," Cathy said. "It's chilly by the ocean."

Philip sank against his pillows. "It's funny, but I get nostalgic in old houses."

"Are you answering my question?"

"Which one?"

"Are we going to live here?"

"I don't know," he said.

"The way Law talked at supper, he desperately wants you to—if you take the job."

"If."

"Isn't it a good job?"

"Very good, considering."

"What would it pay?"

"Ninety-five hundred. That's for two courses."

"It sounds like a lot more than we're used to," she said.

"We'd spend it just as fast."

"I guess." She got into bed; Philip let her take one of the pillows and doubled up the other behind him. "So are you going to take it?"

"We'll talk it over," Philip said, "but let's wait until morning."

Cathy turned onto her stomach and raised herself to her elbows. "You sleepy?"

"No, but I don't want to make decisions."

She turned away from him, pulled out the lamp, and lay flat. After a moment she said: "Law's a funny duck. But he certainly thinks you're the fair-haired boy."

"He's changed some. That thing with the demon or whatever it is on the roof is weird."

"What's that all about, anyway?"

"I'm damned if I know. He might be getting senile—"

"How old is he?"

"He's just past sixty. And then when we were off grave-digging, I couldn't make much sense out of him."

"That poor kitty-cat," she said.

"It isn't your fault."

"But I feel so guilty for letting out that monster dog of theirs."

"Then think about something else."

"He's certainly crazy about that dog, isn't he?"

Philip hesitated. "Robinson means a lot to him," he said.

"What do you think of his wife?"

"She's nice. Aren't *you* sleepy?"

"No," she said. "Don't you want to talk?"

"Not especially."

It was not that he was weighing his answer to Law, or that he had something he badly wanted to think about; he only wished silence for its own sake. Lying on his back under the weight of three quilts, in July, he relaxed. He felt inexplicably peaceful. Through the opened windows he could hear the sea sounds—nothing so rhythmic as the piling up of waves on a shore, but only a long, wind-like whisper—and the calling from distance to distance of land birds behind the old house. There was a moon; he could make out in the dim shadows from its light the planes of walls and ceiling. Everything was as if he belonged here—as if this were, in fact, his grandmother's house, where he had lived most of his childhood. It was almost as if the small girl who just then whimpered in her sleep from the next room were imitating himself. He wondered if she dreamed his dreams, if perhaps the eternity of ocean filtering into her sleep had frightened her the way eternity had once frightened him. He lay tense, ready to go in and comfort her.

But he had been twelve, he remembered, before he began waking up from such dreams. He would lie still, listening to the sounds that inhabited the dark of his room, staring blindly into the ceiling corners, indulging himself in his terror. He had tried then to encompass the universe with his mind, and when he failed he wept and screamed until one of his parents came to his room. Sometimes it was his mother, who sat on the edge of his bed and put her hand to his forehead; he recalled their dialogue:

"What is it, Philip? What's the matter?"

"I'm afraid."

"Of what, dear?"

"I don't know."

"There now, sweetheart, don't cry. Mother's here."

And she would sit by him and stroke his brow and cheeks, and hold his hand until his fear was sobbed out and he had gone back to sleep.

At other times it was his father who came. He sat on the bed, not touching Philip, and he would listen to Philip's tears sometimes for a full minute before speaking:

"What's the trouble, Philip?"

"I'm afraid."

"Is your stomach upset?"

"A little."

"Maybe you'd better go to the bathroom."

Then he got out of bed and went into the bathroom, his father following, and he would sit in that room whose white fixtures and cream-colored walls were dazzling after the dimness of his bedroom. He stopped crying at once, and sat feeling muddled and dizzy with light, and chilled because the hour was late and the heat was off. His father balanced himself on the rim of the bathtub to sit near him, but they exchanged no more words. Philip had more than once stolen a sidewise glance at his father's face, but his father never looked at him as his mother would have. Instead, Father always stared at the tiny white octagons of the tile floor, holding on to the cast-iron rim of the tub so fiercely that the skin over his knuckles was stretched white, and in those moments Philip had known that he was not the only one who was afraid. He loved his father then; he hoped his own child might someday love him as much.

Cathy nudged him. "Listen," she said.

Like a waking from a dream, it was several seconds before Philip could bring his mind to bear on the immediate world. He heard the sound of someone walking over his head.

"It must be Law," he said.

"What's he doing up? They went to bed *hours* ago."

"He was up last night. Is it a crime to have insomnia?"

"No, but it's spooky," she said. "I thought it was that gnome up on the roof."

"Hallucinations don't wear shoes," Philip said.

The footsteps crossed the ceiling, stopped, then resumed on the front staircase, descending.

"He's in the kitchen," Cathy whispered. She was huddled against Philip, both her hands holding his upper arm. "Isn't this loony?"

The noise of Law's walking diminished, vanished.

"Where is he?"

"He must have gone out to the shed."

"He didn't even turn on any *lights*." She took her hands away and stretched out on her stomach. "That's the way very old people act—always prowling around their rooms way early-early in the morning."

"I know," Philip said.

"Listen—is that rain?"

Philip held his breath. He got up and went to the window, then came back to Cathy. "It's nothing," he said.

"What's nothing?"

"Law is peeing; that's all."

"Honestly?" She giggled. "Right out in the open?"

"There's nothing wrong with that, is there?"

"Men are strange," she said. She buried her face in the pillow.

"When I was a kid, I used to go out the attic window."

Cathy gave way to smothered laughter; the bed shook with it. Outside, a hinge creaked. They heard the rattle of wood on wood. A door slapped shut and the report echoed against the clapboards of the house.

Cathy threw her arms around him. "Phil, I can't stand it. I can't spend a whole week here listening to that."

"Why don't you go to sleep?"

"I can't." She kissed his neck and shoulder. "Couldn't we make love a little?"

"Just because you can't sleep?"

"Don't make fun of me." She put her hand down to him. "Please."

"Take it slow," he said. He put his hand over hers and held her from moving. "Listen."

They heard bumping against the eaves.

"It's a ladder."

"My God, Phil, I'll go crazy thinking about this."

"He must be climbing up."

"He'll fall," Cathy said.

"No, no," Philip answered. "You come closer."

She moved. For the next moment her face was pale and featureless before him, over him. He reached out to frame it between his hands, but before he could touch her hair she vanished. The lamp flared suddenly on, blinding him; Cathy was out of bed, plucking her robe from the closet.

"I can't bear it, Phil. His poor wife."

Philip threw back the quilts and got up. "It's none of our business, is it?"

"Just it's scaring me stiff."

"If it makes you happy," Philip said. Something more than irritation informed his actions as he pulled his trousers over his nakedness. Barefoot, he went to the kitchen door and opened it. The room was lighted; Vivian Law was seated at the table, facing him, her hands folded in front of her.

"It's nothing," Vivian said. Her voice was thin. Her gaze, though it was centered on Philip, gave back glassy highlights from the lamp.

"What's the matter with him?" Cathy said over Philip's bare shoulder. "What's he doing out there?"

"It's all right," Vivian repeated. "Please go back to bed."

"We were both a little restless," Philip said, as if he were beginning to make an apology.

"Can I do anything?" Cathy said.

"No, please."

Philip said to Cathy: "Come on, let's get some sleep," but his wife pushed past him into the kitchen. She stopped midway between Philip and Vivian.

"How can you just sit there?" she said. "What if he should fall? What if he should just fall and kill himself?"

Vivian stood up. *Oh, Christ,* Philip thought; *either she will cry or make a speech or slap Cathy's mouth.* Instead, she only put her hands to the collar of her bathrobe and drew its lapels together under her chin; she looked past Cathy at Philip.

"Duncan thinks something is up there," she whispered.

"What is it?" Cathy insisted.

"He doesn't know."

"Why don't you stop him?"

"He has the right to look for himself."

With a small, frustrated cry, Cathy turned and went back to the bedroom. Philip said:

"Do you want me to go out?"

Vivian shook her head.

"Do you want me to wait with you?" He had a sketchy vision of the two of them playing cards at the kitchen table.

"No," she said. "Please."

Philip left her standing in the center of the room and went to bed. He undressed and lay by his wife; she was trembling.

"What does he think he's going to find? What's the matter with him?"

"I can't imagine," Philip said. And yet now he *could* imagine—hearing, faintly, Law's careful progress across the shingles to the peak of the roof—the horror of the man's helpless vision. He knew that every night-sound of his life to come would arouse in him something similar to Law's fear, growing with time closer and closer to fact. After the locking of doors and the look into the nursery, he would lie awake and listen. A murmured question from Cathy would be like some dim message telegraphed from the cellars of this sea; Deborah's dream cries like a mimicry of these whippoorwills; the departing conversation of guests on the porch of a neighbor's home like a dialogue muttered under these eaves. All voices after dark would be the voices of an apparition; Philip imagined himself—uncomfortable, drawing in his breath, raising himself on one elbow—not daring to move lest the rustling of the bedclothes drown out his chance to overhear a secret intelligence from the unlighted world. He would always be afraid that one day he, too, would see an unfamiliar figure, and that one night it would call out his name as it now called Duncan Law's.

Cathy put out the light and lay with her face close to his.

"Please," she said softly, "don't make us live in this terrible, scary place."

"No," Philip said, and he lay still in his wife's embrace. "Did you know he shot Robinson?"

"Law did that? He killed the dog?"

"With a pistol he keeps in the shed."

"Oh, Phil," Cathy said. Her arms around him were rigid. "Oh, God, all you poor, dear men."

Happy Marriages Are All Alike

Archaic offspring of the machines that had barnstormed the 'Twenties, a single-engined biplane circled lazily in the sky above Ruth Bowden. Its presence touched her mind like the drone of a persistent housefly, and when she shielded her eyes to look at it against the glare its remote body showed bottle-green in the sunlight. She closed her eyes and smiled faintly, letting her hand fall to the side of the lawn chair and her knuckles brush the tips of the soft grass.

It was Mickey, her husband, the smile was intended for. It was his plane, with him at the controls, beginning another day of dusting. She slouched in the flimsy chair, her red hair raffish over the plastic back of it, her pale legs stretched straight in front of her. The tiny plane flew out of sight toward the south.

At this early hour of a sultry July morning Ruth felt weak and contented. Because it was Saturday, she was letting the housework go; she had scheduled herself to do nothing until Mickey came home at four. Then she would fix herself up and try to persuade him to take her to dinner and a movie. The day was going to be hot anyway—too hot for any sort of labor. She squirmed. The chair fabric was sharp on the back of her neck, and when she could not finally be comfortable she slid out of the seat and lay flat and relaxed on the cool grass.

Ruth Bowden was twenty-seven. Like many redheads she was not a beautiful woman, but she was pretty in a hazardous way. Her face was a perfect pale oval, but the delicate skin flushed deeply and easily from heat, from excitement, from exertion. She burned readily and took finicky care not to spend too much time in the sun. Though her hair was richly burnt orange, her eyebrows were light and most of her make-up time she spent penciling them in. Her mouth, full and with a prominent lower lip, was always chapped; she had to use prescription lipstick.

She realized—and she was frequently told—that her eyes were her best feature. They were green tending toward yellow, luminous and reflective like a cat's. Green was Mickey's favorite color; he had fallen in love with her for her eyes.

That was seven years earlier, in Texas. She was a junior at A & I, and one spring evening a gang of the students had driven to Matamoros. In that foreign place, at a nightclub with an outdoor dance floor, and with the noise of a mambo band brassy in her ears, she had met and danced with Mickey Bowden. Now she could only remember that he had dazzled her. He was much older than she, he had been a fighter pilot in a war she had scarcely read about, he talked earnestly about things she had never dreamed of—and he walked with a limp. She was justly dazzled, she thought, and at the same time she was—providentially—saved.

By the age of twenty, Ruth Clay had already drifted in and out of a half-dozen casual affairs with older men. What she lacked in beauty she made up for in eagerness, and with her arrival at college she became an amateur of the passions. Marriage did not concern her, nor was she only fond of sex; it was the illicitness of her adventures that most excited her. Breaking the college rules, deceiving the guest registers of motels—being above the law—was the thrill for her.

Her liaisons never survived one or two animal weekends along the highway outside Kingsville, and then the novelty was worn off. She came back to the rooming house where she lived, slept twelve or fourteen hours, then dropped easily back into the routine of classes and clubs. Her friends asked about her absences; she told them as many details as she could remember, and if her friends happened to know the man she listened with a feline smile as they praised his looks, or his clothes, or his money. It was like hearing interesting fiction; her own knowledge of her lovers was restricted to fundamentals.

Mickey was not like her other men, and not like her. From the first night in Matamoros he seemed unconcerned with sex or excitement. He told Ruth he was attracted to her, but because he liked her as a dancing partner—because she made him feel at ease despite his limp. He bought her drinks, but did not encourage her; he did not need her to be drunk. When the night ended he was entirely willing that she leave with her school crowd. He did ask to see her again in Kingsville.

They went out several evenings a week on Coke dates, Mickey calling for her at the rooming house in a vintage Plymouth and being careful to return her before midnight, the latest sign-out hour she was allowed. Ruth did not object to his slowness—the most he permitted himself was a good-night kiss—and with time she found pleasure in his lesser attentions. It became a new gratification for her to stop short of bed with a man; she was content when she was with Mickey to listen to his stories and to admire in his face the age lines like a movie hero's. Her motel adventures came to an end, and her friends engaged her in brisk discussions on the subject of her surprise reformation.

At that time Mickey was working in Corpus Christi, flying for a crop-dusting service. The job took him up and down most of the Rio Grande Valley, and there were times, if he was called to West Texas, when Ruth did not see him for two and three weeks. His was a life she considered glamorous, and the glamour was confirmed for her that summer when Mickey let her fly with him. She fell in love with his plane—the clumsy machine that shuddered against the strength of its engine and whistled in flight like wind through bare trees. It was high pleasure for her to sit in an open cockpit, feeling speed on her face and watching the flat farmlands hurtle past only a few yards beneath her. When she looked back, the sickly white insect spray was funneling down into a heavy blanket over cotton and vegetables, and she flattered herself that she was the goddess assigned to construct clouds.

Mickey proposed at the end of the summer, and she accepted him as much for the exhilaration of the one flight as from love of the man. He had not asked her to come flying with him since, either in

Albany, New York, where they moved after the wedding, or here in Connecticut. She always hoped he would, feeling that his occupation made them different from other couples and held out to them the chance to share something unusual. Ruth believed she was well married, and she did not mind her apparent inability to have children, but she often found herself longing for some equivalent to the risks of her single days.

She continued to draw vicarious and even desperate satisfaction from Mickey's flying. Her moments of purest delight came on those occasional afternoons when, at the end of his working day, Mickey buzzed their small house on his way to the airfield. She would hear his plane approaching from the south and run out to the wide, open lawn to wait for it, her forehead flushed from the anticipation. It came into sight high over the trees across the road, and she would know Mickey had seen her when the plane began its long, shallow glide toward her. As it came closer she spread her arms and laughed into the deep flutter of the engine, as if she were offering herself to the machine. It was a thrill as great as any she had ever known when the black silhouette, almost on her, suddenly broke off its descent and banked away to the northeast with the roar of full throttle, the backwash from its propeller rustling the leaves of the surrounding trees and sometimes laying a caress of warm air across her face. Once, playfully, Mickey had contrived to cover the yard with a brief cloud of insecticide; its odor had been aphrodisiac to her, and when he had flown on she fell on the grass beside the patio and waited in a kind of absurd ecstasy for him to come home.

Flying for a pest control company was not like flying combat missions for the Air Corps, but at forty-one Mickey Bowden had resigned himself to the tamer life. His biplane—patched and wired, and hungry for activity like some retired hunting dog—was his last real connection to a past he often turned back to in his thoughts. Circling now at fifteen hundred feet above the lush Connecticut hills so that his wife could look up and see he was airborne, free of the earth, he had at least a facsimile of the release he had used to feel in England and in Texas when he was arrogant about the silver pilot's wings over his breast pocket.

He had bought the plane in 1949, shortly after his release from the military, with his discharge money and the combat pay he had managed to save and invest after the war. The craft was God only knew how ancient. Yet it did its job; it had paid for itself several times; it would go on, clunker though it was, until some remote day when Mickey would give up his flying. There was no guessing when that day would come for him.

He had always loved airplanes. He had built them as a boy, soloed at his hometown field in Virginia when he was seventeen, been top man in his flight class at Randolph during the war. By the time he arrived in England in 1943, he already had the reputation of a hot pilot, and more than a hundred missions over France and Germany had confirmed it. He flew a P-51 Mustang, sometimes on cover missions to places like Bremen and Hamburg, sometimes on strafing missions to the Continent. It was these last he loved best. After D-Day, when the German forces began their slow retreat, Mickey turned down passes and rest leaves in order to miss no chance to tear up the convoys and lines of infantry along the muddy French roads. He enjoyed a madman's notoriety among his friends and flying partners.

He was never really wounded, never shot down, but he won a Purple Heart when he ran out of fuel over Belgium during the war's last winter. His plane crash-landed; frostbite cost him the toes on his right foot. It was a humiliating decoration for him, and he did not wear it.

After the war he stayed in uniform. He was shipped back to Randolph as an instructor in basic pilot training, and he hung on there, fighting his boredom as best he could, until a war comrade wrote and invited him to join a crop-dusting outfit in Corpus Christi. Mickey resigned his commission, bought his rickety plane, and took the job. He bore no grudge against peace, but he had known only one truly happy moment since the close of the war in Europe. He was asked to fly one of the old Mustangs against a pair of jet fighters in an air-show demonstration whose object was to dramatize the superiority of the new jets. He accepted; he even had the satisfaction of outmaneuvering the two younger pilots for the first few minutes of the mock dog-fight. In the end he had felt like a fool, as obsolete as the aircraft he flew.

Civilian life brought him no salvations. He made good money, he had an easy job, his war experiences made him—among other aptitudes—an easy master of seduction. By the time he met Ruth Clay in Mexico, he had decided he was ready to put down roots; it was a compromise he had been fending off for several years, and he recognized even then that stability was a cast of life which would probably not make him happy. During the Korean War—when the Air Force had denied his recommission—Mickey took his pleasure from the newsreels, living secondhand the action photographed by the wing cameras of the jets. Now he watched the war movies revived on television, and sometimes he went with Ruth to a drive-in theater rerun.

Because of his capitulation to calm, Mickey's relationship with Ruth followed a pattern different from his earlier encounters with women. He began by according her a respect he was not sure she deserved. To her he told his stories with the aim of persuading her that he was mature enough—he was then thirty-four—to marry. He admired her dancing and her personality; he assured her she was pretty, and that he liked her eyes. In all the time he spent courting her he never once suggested—and rarely thought about—making love. Once he had taken her flying with him, but though she appeared to enjoy it he resolved not to repeat the invitation. It was not the same as being alone; he felt repressed, prevented from taking the small but important chances that once in a while made his day better than usual.

He had not minded the wedding. The event gave him the opportunity to collect a half-dozen friends he had not seen since 1945, and his bachelor party the night before the marriage was an alcoholic reprise of the Battle of Europe. The ceremony was an anticlimax. He and Ruth spent a week's honeymoon in Houston, shopped and rode buses during the day, made a professional sort of love at night. These beginnings did not much comfort Mickey, nor did the years that followed. He had thought Ruth to be a little wilder than she turned out; he had half-counted on a family to distract him from his boredom.

The Bowdens had moved twice since their marriage. First they had gone to New York for a job with the state's forest service. Mickey was on a fire patrol, and all during a damp summer he saw no fires and quit his job with awkward apologies to his employers. From there he had taken the position in Connecticut. Ruth was happy in the last move; she appreciated the status of living in suburban surroundings. Mickey was neither happy nor unhappy. This was, simply, another place to pass the time. Sometimes he dusted crops, sometimes he sprayed for communities whose town councils had voted insect control. He sustained himself—as now, heading his plane down the Connecticut Valley for the day's work—with the thought that at least he was flying, and at least when he was flying he was free.

Late that afternoon Ruth was in the bedroom, selecting a cool dress for the movies, when she heard the faint murmur of Mickey's plane. She pushed the closet door shut and ran down the hall to the front of the house. Outside on the lawn, straining her eyes to the south, she picked out the tiny plane high over the trees in the near distance, and she waved her arms, hoping by so weak a semaphore to remind Mickey of how long it had been since he had pleased her by buzzing the house. Almost as soon as she waved the plane began losing altitude, sliding down the sultry sky toward her, growing larger and louder.

Neither of them realized the pleasure each was about to give the other. Mickey could not have understood the raw, animal delight that informed his wife's spread-eagled pose in the green yard ahead of his machine; and Ruth could not have guessed how, inside the cockpit, her husband was crouched forward, sighting along the cowl, pretending she was a Nazi staff officer surprised outside his quarters—and that the shuddering in the wings of his aged aircraft came from the murderous hammering of his six .50 caliber machine guns.